Hold Me:
Brie's Submission

By
Red Phoenix

Hold Me: Brie's Submission

Copyright © 2016 by Red Phoenix
Print Edition

RedPhoenix69@live.com

Edited by Amy Parker, Proofed by Becki Wyer and Marilyn Cooper
Cover by CopperLynn
Phoenix symbol by Nicole Delfs

*Previously published as part of *Brie Embraces the Heart of Submission*
Adult Reading Material (18+)

Dedication

Thanks to my husband and my children
for putting up with the long hours it takes to release
these stories from my head.
Your love and support means everything to me!

Thanks as well to my parents,
my two cousins (enthusiastic fans),
and
my brother and his wife,
for standing beside me.

As always, love to my beautiful fans!

CONTENTS

Confronting the Beast

Although she had been tempted to stay with Lea, it had been Mary's no-nonsense advice she'd needed. She'd warned Brie not to take the letter but, naturally, Brie had refused to listen. Well, she was listening now.

Mary gave Brie no sympathy, even remarking that it would be good if Sir uncollared her. When Brie broke down in hysterical tears at the suggestion, Mary quickly changed the subject.

"All you can do now is prove to Sir you understand you were wrong, and do whatever it takes to earn his trust back. If he wants to be done, then be a woman about it and leave with dignity. After all, you're the one who screwed up."

Brie struggled to breathe, unable to bear the thought of losing Sir.

Mary took pity on her. "But if he knows you at all, he'll understand that you were only trying to help."

"I was, Mary! That was my only motivation," Brie cried.

"Yeah, yeah… Good intentions or not, the simple

fact is you disobeyed him on something deeply personal. He has every right to be angry. You have to accept what comes, Brie, and deal with it. Don't be a whiny baby about it."

But the idea of life without Sir killed Brie inside. "I can't lose him! Don't you understand that he's everything to me?"

Mary stared at her without a lick of sympathy. "If he would be happier without you, would you really deny him that?"

Brie crumpled into a heap on the couch. "No…"

"Then rest tonight. Be strong for your Master tomorrow. He'll need your positive energy, even if he dismisses you after the meeting."

Brie looked up at Mary, a sureness of spirit slowly taking over as she sat up straight. "Yes, you're right. I created this mess; it is my duty to see him through it."

Mary nudged Brie's shoulder with her hip. "So go to bed and make me proud tomorrow."

Brie woke up, steeling herself for the difficult meeting. Ruth was a dangerous person—indifferent of others on a level that was terrifying.

She called Sir at exactly noon, afraid to hear the displeasure in his voice. It only rang once before he answered. His tone was formal and distant. "Where are you?"

"At Mary's, Sir."

"Expect me in twenty minutes." He hung up before she could respond.

She looked at Mary. "He's still pissed."

"To be honest, Brie, he probably isn't thinking of you. All of his focus is centered on navigating this meeting with the bitch. I only have to imagine how I would be if I was meeting my father to know how Sir feels."

Brie found solace in that. "My job is to serve as his strength."

"There's no need to wish you luck, then. You will succeed in that, I'm sure of it."

Brie felt only gratitude. "Thanks, Mary. You've given me exactly what I needed to survive this nightmare."

"A nightmare you created," Mary pointed out, in typical Blonde Nemesis fashion.

Brie waited for Sir outside. She had planned to jump into the Lotus when it pulled up, but Sir insisted on getting out and opening the door for her. It gave her some hope that he could find it in his heart to forgive her.

The ride was silent except for a few simple instructions. "Do not speak directly to her."

"Yes, Sir."

"Do not accept anything she says as truth. She is a master of manipulation."

"Understood, Sir."

"Keep out of my way."

"I will say and do nothing, Sir, unless you ask."

He turned to stare at her briefly. "I do not want you there. It is another power play I must endure, but it will not go unanswered." He hit the steering wheel with a vengeance, but said no more for the rest of the drive.

Sir pulled up to a high-end hotel and threw the keys to the valet without a word. He helped Brie out of the car and led her through the doors robotically. The vacant look in his eyes alerted her to the fact that his mind was elsewhere.

Naturally, Ruth was staying at the penthouse suite. Sir grunted his displeasure when the bellman pressed the button. The ride up was tense—even the young man sensed the gravity of their mood and coughed several times to hide his discomfort.

The elevator doors opened onto a small hallway and a two-door entry. Sir put his hand on Brie's back and guided her out of the elevator, then rang the doorbell without hesitation.

"Let yourself in," Ruth called from inside.

Sir waited until the elevator closed before opening the door. "Stay beside me," he commanded softly. They entered the spacious loft and he shut the massive doors behind them.

Ruth was lying on a red velvet couch in a flowing gown, looking every bit the part of a diva. "Right on time, like a good boy."

"Where's the violin?"

"No, son, not so fast. We need to talk first."

"Produce the violin or I will leave."

Ruth narrowed her eyes, studying him for a second before pulling herself off the couch and disappearing into the bedroom. She came back a few moments later, holding the violin away from her as if it were a piece of unwanted trash.

She laid it on the end of the sofa, placed a pillow over it and lay back down, her body a shield protecting the instrument. "Now we will talk. Take a seat," she said, gesturing to a small couch opposite hers. "Both of you."

Sir led Brie over and they sat down, facing Ruth, but Brie turned her head and stared at Sir's chest. She concentrated all her energies upon his heart.

"She's a mousey little thing, isn't she?" Ruth complained.

"I'm not here to discuss Miss Bennett. Why don't you just state your request and be done with the games?"

Ruth's laughter filled the room. "Request? It's a demand, son. Make no mistake about it. Desperate times call for desperate measures."

Brie saw Sir's lips twitch, but he said calmly, "Proceed."

"It's simple. I have plenty of cash overseas, but am temporarily unable to access it and I need it now. The only way I can survive this cancer is through non-traditional means. That takes money and lots of it, son."

"Are we still imagining we have cancer?"

Her voice became low and harsh. "You are a heartless bastard. Yes, I'm dying! But I see that has no effect on you."

When she got no response from Sir, she addressed Brie. "What kind of son treats his dying mother this way?"

Brie continued to stare at Sir's chest, but she felt a slow, angry blush creep over her face.

"Now you can see what a ruthless man he truly is.

But at least you believe me, Brie. You've been on my side from the beginning and even helped me meet with him today. You're really precious to me, dear. You know that, don't you?"

When Brie did not answer, she laughed. "Thane, she reminds me of your father. That look of pure devotion…it will be the death of her."

"Enough!" he snapped.

"Mark my words, you will destroy her. You are, after all, your mother's son."

Sir stood up. "We're done here."

Ruth lay back on the couch. "No, we're not. There's still the issue of the money for my cancer treatment."

"How much?"

"It isn't cheap. It could run as high as a million."

"I don't have that amount of money lying around," he stated angrily.

"Well, then give it to me in installments. Half a million now, half a million before Brie's film comes out."

"Why then?"

"Insurance."

Sir pulled out his checkbook, calmly wrote out a check for five hundred thousand dollars from his personal account and held it out to her.

Brie felt sick to her stomach watching him give in so easily to the witch.

"Have Brie bring it to me, boy."

Sir gave the check to Brie and nodded, his eyes revealing neither anger nor defeat. She stood up and walked over to Ruth. The woman lay there, studying her like a piece of meat. With a dissatisfied grunt, she took the check. "Before I give her the violin, let me make sure this money is good."

She called the number on the check and verified the funds were available.

"Good boy." She sat up and pulled the violin from under the pillow. She held it out to Brie and, without warning, dropped it from her grasp.

With lightning-quick reflexes, Brie caught the instrument before it hit the floor.

"Pity," the woman exclaimed, folding the check and stuffing it into her brassiere.

Brie carried the violin with reverence back to Sir. He took it, looking it over briefly before commenting. "Do you have the case?"

"It's in the bedroom. Have your pet get it," Ruth answered in a disinterested voice.

With Sir's permission, Brie went to retrieve it. The case, lined with red velvet, was open on the bed. She closed it slowly, feeling power radiating from that simple violin case—a connection to the past.

Brie held it to her chest as she walked back to Sir. With the same reverence she had shown, Sir placed the violin inside and latched it shut.

Sir spoke to Ruth in a businesslike manner. "Where should I send the next check? I do not want to meet with you again."

"Agreed. Totally unnecessary to meet in person. I've gotten what I need from my heartless son." She lifted a card from the table and handed it to him. "Send it here two weeks before the premiere. Failure to do so will have dire consequences."

Sir took the card and tucked it into his jacket.

"There are three things you might find of interest, Ruth." He nodded towards the check. "One: that is a bogus account. You will not be receiving any funds from me. Two: I know that you had your medical records altered. I could only wish to get rid of you that easily. Three: my lawyer informed me that you are bankrupt—not a cent to your name. You are living on borrowed time and that time has finally run out."

She rose from the couch in a furious rage. "Foolish boy! I will *bury* you!"

Sir tucked the violin under his arm and said, "We're finished here."

"Finished is right!" Ruth screeched. "My threats are not idle, Thane. I will trash your reputation as thoroughly as I did your father's. You will lose everything. Money, honor…" she looked directly at Brie, "…love."

"Unlike my father, I am not dead and can defend myself."

Her laughter was hard and cruel. "You underestimate me, son. There will be nothing left when I'm through."

"I repeat, I am capable of defending myself. And yes, your threats *are* idle. I do not fear you." He put his hand on Brie's back and directed her towards the door.

Ruth hissed from behind them, "I'm coming after you too, precious. If I don't ruin you, Thane will."

Brie took a deep breath once the elevator doors had closed. It felt as if she had survived a physical battle. She was exhausted, both emotionally and physically. She glanced at Sir and was heartened to see a slight smirk on his face.

Yes, he'd won the hour.

Although Sir remained aloof when they returned home, he called her to him that evening and asked her to bow at his feet. "I actually contemplated uncollaring you, Brie, but something the beast said today caused me to reconsider. She is correct in likening your devotion to that of my father. It is also true that a part of my mother lives in me. I am capable of being heartless and cruel, but my father's unfailing passion beats in this heart. It is his legacy that I choose to live out."

Brie looked up hesitantly, afraid to hope.

"Are you repentant of reading the letter?"

"More than you know, Sir."

"Will you ever contact her again, in any way?"

"Never knowingly, Sir."

He snorted in understanding and amended his statement. "Will you immediately tell me if you encounter her unexpectedly?"

"Immediately, Sir. No hesitation."

He ordered her to stand. "As punishment, I could have you endure another session with rice or even a thorough beating."

Brie bowed her head, ready to accept his punishment, although she feared it would be much harsher than the first.

His breath was long and drawn out, as if he was completely exhausted. "However, I fear whatever the beast has planned will far surpass any punishment I could deliver. She will attempt to break you emotionally. It will get ugly, I guarantee it. Are you strong enough? If not, then I should set you free now."

She took offense at the offer and stated proudly, "I would die for you, Sir."

He growled, "Dying is not an option, téa."

Hearing her pet name uttered from his lips made her whole body sing with relief. "What I meant, Sir, is that I would suffer any hardship to remain by your side."

"You must be sure, téa."

Brie kissed his hand lovingly. "In good times and in bad, there is no place I would rather be than by your side."

"Then we stand together."

"As one, Sir."

His smirk from earlier returned. "I did enjoy the look on her face the moment she realized she'd been beaten at her own game."

"It was brilliantly delivered, Sir."

"After being forced into a corner, I spent the night devising my plan and setting the wheels in motion. As my mother said, 'Desperate times call for desperate measures.' The beast didn't stand a chance."

"Your father would have been proud."

"No," Sir said solemnly, "he would have been saddened that we were still fighting against each other, but I trust he'd have understood my actions." His gaze suddenly became sentimental. "Although I was against you being there today, your presence was…appreciated."

Brie smiled at him lovingly.

Sir took her hand and placed it over the healing brand on his chest. "This is where you remain. Always."

Burying herself in his embrace, she whispered, "Thank you, Sir."

When she walked into the bedroom that night, she found the violin lying in the middle of the bed. The two lay down on either side of it. She could tell he had something he wanted to share.

Sir touched the strings, making a light strumming sound. "This instrument has been in our family for over two hundred years. It was passed down from generation to generation to the most promising talent."

"I had no idea it was that old."

"My great-grandfather was an American who fought in World War I. He fell in love with the Italian language and culture after making friends among the troops and decided to relocate there after the war ended. He married the sister of one of his Italian comrades and set about propagating the world with eight children, the youngest being my grandfather. Although *Nonno* never stepped onto American soil, he carried the Davis name and was granted the family heirloom when it was discovered his son had exceptional talent."

Brie stroked the smooth wood, amazed so much family history was represented in one instrument.

"My American relatives invested in his education, flying my father out here when he was only twelve. For all intents and purposes, he grew up an American but never lost his love for his homeland. At least four times a year we would visit, even when his concert schedule became hectic. Family meant everything to him."

"What a rich childhood you had, Sir."

"True, I did." His eyes held a haunted look, but Sir smiled as he looked down at the violin. "After he passed, the only thing I wanted of my father's was this violin. Naturally, my mother refused to give it to me. I had assumed she'd sold it because of its considerable worth, but now I realize she kept it all these years for one reason."

Brie looked at him sadly. "Blackmail."

His eyes narrowed and his voice became dark. "Yes, but she failed to take into account that I *am* my mother's son. I am not so easily manipulated."

Brie ran her fingers over the strings tenderly. "Now it's back where it belongs." She smiled. "Is this the violin he always played, Sir?"

His expression softened. "Yes. My father would touch no other."

"So when I hear his music, I am hearing this instrument."

"Yes."

"Wow…" she said in admiration. Brie looked at it again, realizing it was a piece of Alonzo's soul in physical form.

Sir picked it up and placed it back in the case. "And now it can wait for the next in the Davis line to bring it back to life."

"A beautiful gift…"

His eyes shone with triumph when he replied, "A valuable legacy. One worth fighting for."

Excitement at The Haven

Brie's Master was asked to join an impromptu meeting at The Haven with several of the other Submissive Training Center staff members. The discussion was to center on issues anticipated following the publicizing of the documentary. Sir had given Brie permission to roam the club until he had finished.

Sir was no longer worried about Faelan. After the formal meeting with the Dom, Brie had had no further trouble with him. It seemed Faelan had found his niche in the community with a little guidance from Marquis, and he was highly popular at the club these days.

From what Brie could gather from information Lea had shared, he had created an unusual routine at The Haven, inspired by the auctions at the Center. At the start of each evening, submissives were invited to fill out a form detailing a simple fantasy they wanted to play out that particular night. An hour before he was scheduled to scene, Faelan would announce the scenario that had captured his interest. The lucky sub would then spread the word, guaranteeing a large audience to watch it.

It was not only popular with the subs, but with fellow Dominants as well. They took the opportunity to observe the wide variety of scenes presented and select those that aroused them to recreate at home. Despite Faelan's young age, he was a master of role play and displayed advanced skills, having been trained by both Sir and Marquis. It made him a hot commodity in the community.

Although Sir no longer considered Faelan a threat, he reminded her, "If at any point you feel uncomfortable, seek Tono out. He has been made aware that I will be in a meeting tonight."

As Brie watched Sir walk off to join Headmaster Coen and Master Anderson, she felt a thrill. She hadn't been allowed this kind of freedom in forever, and she found it invigorating.

She stepped over to the first alcove and was surprised to find Marquis finishing a scene. Celestia, his collared sub, was bound to a wooden St. Andrew's cross, her back a crisscross of red marks, indicating that she'd received an intense flogging from him.

Marquis zipped up the bag that held his infamous tools. He approached his sub with predatory grace, turning her head and kissing her forcefully while she was still bound.

Celestia's moan resonated in Brie's core. It was the sound of a woman who had been flying high in subspace, brought back to earth by the overwhelming connection of her Master's kiss.

She heard him say faintly, "My beautiful star…"

Her eyes fluttered open and she smiled. "My heart."

Brie was moved by their simple exchange. She admired how each D/s couple had their own erotic dance. No two couples followed the exact same steps, but the deep level of trust and respect was consistent throughout the community.

Marquis released Celestia from the cross and cradled her in his arms, kissing her lightly. It was the romantic side of Marquis that Brie had been surprised by the first time she'd scened with him during training.

She smiled to herself, remembering the first day she'd met him at the Training Center. Oh, how Marquis Gray had frightened her with his dark, penetrating eyes and ghostlike figure. She understood now that looks did not define a person. It was one of many lessons she'd learned at the Center.

Brie quietly moved on to the next scene, wanting to give them privacy to bask in their aftercare.

At the next alcove she came across a Master punishing his slave. Brie had no idea what her offense had been, but he commanded his naked slave to mold herself to the 'Pole of Penance'. The girl walked over to the sleek metal pole and turned around to face the crowd, her face the picture of repentance.

Attached to the pole was a thick, black dildo. The slave bent over and pressed her ass against the toy. The multitudes watched as the girl began rocking against the large, latex cock. Her Master stood over her, obviously enjoying the sight of the dark phallus penetrating his sub. He grunted, stroking his cock as he watched.

The slave whimpered occasionally as she willingly ground against the toy, forcing it deeper into her ass.

"Hands above your head, slave," he ordered when the penetration was complete. He then tied her hands to a ring and pulled the rope taut. Brie could imagine how the girl must feel, with her body stretched by the binding and her ass stretched by the large toy inside her. Then her Master added a new element—the Magic Wand.

Brie whimpered along with her.

He held it in front of his slave, stating, "Disobedient slaves do not get the pleasure of orgasm."

The girl watched with a look of fear, knowing she was in trouble as he knelt down and bound the wand between her legs, securing it tightly against her clit.

"Please—no, Master," she begged.

Her Master's smile was playfully ruthless. "Do not orgasm or you will meet a much worse fate, slave."

The girl cried out when he switched it on. Brie knew the wand would be creating a delicious vibration between her thighs, and wondered how the girl could possibly hold out. When he turned the wand up to the higher setting, Brie decided to leave. Watching orgasm denial was almost as bad as experiencing it herself.

She moved on, looking for Lea, but stopped short when she saw Boa beginning a scene with his Mistress. He was dressed in black leather chaps and nothing else. His Mistress was wearing embroidered, royal purple silks wrapped tightly around her sleek body, her lips a matching deep plum.

Brie was surprised to see there were four men, including Boa, involved in the scene. It was quite unusual. Boa's Asian Mistress was in charge, so Brie assumed all four males and the one lone female must be submissives.

She forgot all about Lea as she watched the tantalizing scene play out before her.

The girl was ordered to lie on a thin wooden bench. She was bound to it with violet ropes, one just under her breasts and a second binding across her hip bones. Brie noted that her head and pussy were positioned at the edges on either side of the bench. The furniture seemed to be specifically designed for fucking a sub at both ends.

Ingenious.

Brie was a little curious, though, because the girl's hands had been left untied. She looked at the other male submissives and noted that they were wearing similar leather chaps to Boa's. All four men had full erections; however, it was Boa's that drew Brie's attention. She'd never forgotten the challenge of taking his massive cock into her small frame. Just thinking about it now caused a deep ache in her loins.

The Domme grabbed a leather crop and walked over to the girl. "You are about to be banged by my four men. I expect you to please each one equally. I will correct you if necessary." She snapped the crop onto the girl's mound. The sub cried out in pain at the unexpected warning. "That's right. Mistress will be very strict tonight. I want my boys pleased."

"I understand, Mistress Luo," the female answered.

The Asian Domme walked up to each male individually and grabbed his scrotum, squeezing her long nails into his flesh. She leaned in close to his ear, to whisper something the crowd was not privileged to hear.

When she was done, the four men took their places: Boa between the girl's legs, the twins on either side of her and the remaining one at her head. The idea of pleasing all four men at the same time was both frightening and exciting to Brie. Boa was enough of a challenge on his own, and Brie wondered how the sub felt about her task.

She glanced between the girl's legs and noticed her outer lips were already red and swollen, indicating a very turned-on subbie. Brie had long since realized that a woman's vocalizations were never as reliable as the state of her sex.

A female could fake a scream of pleasure, but not an amorous pussy.

The Domme ordered, "Please the twins."

The sub immediately took a cock in each hand and expertly stroked the lengths of their shafts with an added rotation of her wrists at the end. Both men groaned in appreciation of her evident skill.

"Keep them satisfied, sub. Do not slow down, not even for an instant."

"Yes, Mistress Luo. It will be my pleasure."

The Mistress turned to Boa with a hungry look. "Boa, fuck the girl."

Brie bit her bottom lip as she watched the male sub position his colossal shaft against the sub's opening and then grab onto her thighs. The girl panted and groaned as he forced the impossibly large head of his shaft inside her.

Brie felt a trickle down the inside of her own leg. Oh, yes, her pussy knew well the sexy demand of Boa's shaft. She squeezed her legs together, feeling her clit faintly pulse with desire.

While he was still forcing himself inside, the Domme trailed the crop slowly up the girl's body, all the way to her throat and up to her chin. She smiled down at the female and said, "Lex, fuck her pretty mouth."

Brie shivered. She remembered the time she'd been on the doctor's table and Master Harris had deep-throated her while stimulating her clit with a vibrator. That was nothing compared to this. Brie stood glued in place, completely entranced by Mistress Luo's scene.

Lex began by massaging the girl's neck as he slowly eased his shaft past the back of her throat, but there was a moment of instinctual resistance and the girl momentarily paused the motions of her hands.

As promised, Boa's Mistress snapped the crop across her right breast.

The girl twitched on the bench, but she resumed the rapid hand movements even as she whimpered around Lex's cock.

It took time for the girl's muscles to relax enough to take the entire length of Boa's manhood, but Brie found it extremely sexy to watch the process—to see that huge cock force its way in.

Boa's Mistress walked around the scene, complimenting her male subs as she used the leather tab of the crop to caress the female. When the base of Boa's cock was pressed firmly against the girl's mound, the Domme asked, "Are you ready to come, boys?"

All four men answered in unison, "Yes, Mistress."

She leaned down and spoke directly to the girl. "You have done well, sub. This Mistress is pleased. Now it's time to enjoy the fruits of your labor."

The Domme stood up, slapping the crop against her

hand as she announced, "I will count down from ten."

Brie was familiar with that technique—waiting to orgasm until the counting was complete. However, she had never seen it done with multiple partners before. Were they all so well trained that they would come as a unit?

She watched in fascination, holding her breath as the last few numbers were called out. "Four... Three... Two... One."

Boa shuddered deep inside the girl at the same time as Lex, while the twins covered her breasts with large amounts of come. Brie could hear the girl's muffled screams as the two men finished off deep inside her. Suddenly, the female stiffened and her whole body began to shake violently in a powerful orgasm of her own.

All four men stepped away at the same time and allowed their Mistress to approach the girl. "Delicious to watch," she commended. She looked up at the audience, which responded with appreciative applause.

The girl looked up at the Domme with half-hooded eyes, her chest still rising and falling rapidly as she recovered.

"Was it all you had hoped for?" the Domme asked, tracing the end of the crop around the young woman's breasts.

In a hoarse whisper, the girl replied, "Better...Mistress Luo."

"Good," she said soothingly.

Having watched the scene to completion, Brie decided to make her way to the bar, hoping to find Lea there—after a quick trip to the bathroom to rid herself of her soaked panties.

The Wolf Bares His Heart

S he found not only Lea at the bar, but Mary as well. They were sitting together in an intense conversation. As Brie approached, she was startled to spot Faelan standing nearby, casually drinking a beer. Brie passed by him, wondering if he would cause a commotion. But, true to form, the Wolf completely ignored her.

Lea lifted her purse off the empty stool between the two as soon as she saw Brie. "Dang, girl, you finally made it!"

"Sorry, I was watching a scene with Boa and couldn't pull myself away."

Lea grinned. "Oh, that Boa is one fine sub. I've had the pleasure of his cock on several occasions. It's like the first time every session because he's so freaking huge."

Mary interrupted, "Boa Shmoa. Let's get back to talking about Master O."

"Who?" Brie asked.

Lea looked at her in disbelief. "Haven't you heard? Master O is in town tonight."

Brie shrugged her shoulders, the name meaning

nothing to her.

Mary explained, "He's a world-renowned master of blood play…" When she saw that Brie was still clueless, she seemed irritated. "Seriously, you didn't know he's coming to tour the club tonight?"

Brie looked around and noticed the unusually high number of eligible subs parading about. "Is that the reason this place is so packed?"

"Ah…yeah!" Lea teased. "Subs from all over California have come tonight, hoping he'll choose one of them to play out a scene."

They quickly brought Brie up to speed. Apparently, Master O was from Eastern Africa and had traveled the world in order to refine his unique skills. Mary claimed his work with needles was unsurpassed. "You would not believe the artful displays he can create using human skin as his canvas."

Even Lea, who wasn't a fan of blood play, was excited. "I really want to see his work up close. What I've seen in photos is amazing, and don't you just *love* his name?"

"What? Is it in reference to orgasms or something?" Brie asked.

"No, idiot," Mary snapped. "The 'O' stands for type O blood."

Brie laughed. "Aw… Well, that does make him sound a little more dangerous and less conceited."

Lea handed her a drink before asking, "Would you let him scene with you if Sir allowed it?"

"No way. I hate needles. But I wouldn't mind watching…I think." She shuddered involuntarily.

Lea turned to Mary. "What about you?"

Mary rolled her eyes. "Do you even have to ask?"

Brie noticed that Faelan shifted uncomfortably behind Mary. Was it possible he was jealous of Mary's stated interest in the visiting Dom?

"With so many subs to choose from, I wonder which one he'll select. This is going to be fun!" Lea squealed.

Brie grinned at her best friend. "What? Are you hoping he'll pick you?"

"Hey, I wouldn't turn the man down if he asked, but I can't say blood really turns me on, unlike some freaks I know," Lea replied, looking straight at Mary.

Blonde Nemesis snorted. "I wear the 'freak' title gladly. I'm the only truly adventurous one in our little group, Lea the Lackluster." She slapped Brie's back. "Hey, I've got to pee. Watch my stuff." She disappeared into the sea of people without looking back.

Faelan came up from behind and nonchalantly picked up Mary's purse, setting it on the counter in front of him before taking her seat and ordering another beer. The bartender slid it across the counter, where it landed perfectly in Faelan's open hand. He picked up the mug and took a long, hard stare at Brie before giving her a slight nod and tipping the mug to drink.

"So you're acknowledging Brie all of a sudden," Lea commented.

Faelan looked as if he were contemplating ignoring the question, but finally answered, "I'm moving forward."

Brie held up her glass to Faelan. "I'm glad to hear it, Mr. Wallace."

He glanced in the direction Mary had gone and stated, "People don't give that woman the respect she deserves, but that's about to change."

Is Faelan actually being protective of Mary? Brie couldn't believe it. "I agree; she deserves to be treated better."

He corrected, "What she deserves is for people to recognize the extraordinary woman she is and treat her accordingly."

Lea smiled into her glass as she sipped her drink. "Okay…"

Faelan took a long draught of beer and slammed the mug on the counter. "Do you realize that she's the only person since that car crash, all those fucking years ago, who actually cares about me as a man?"

Lea slammed her drink down, imitating him, and stated, "You have *tons* of girls at your beck and call, Faelan."

"I'm not talking about simple fucking, Lea," he growled.

He turned to Brie and stared at her with those intense blue eyes. "After the accident, the boy's family condemned me, and my family and friends have treated me with kid gloves ever since. I don't need sympathy, damn it! What I needed was a taste of reality. Well, Mary is all about shooting you between the eyes with reality."

Brie had to force herself not to smile. "That's one way to put it."

For some odd reason, Faelan seemed to be feeling unusually talkative. Brie gave Lea a little wink when he continued of his own accord, "She and I have struggled with demons from our pasts, believing if we could defeat them we would be free. But that isn't how it works."

Faelan suddenly had Brie's attention. He wasn't spewing some frivolous bullshit just to be heard—he was speaking from the heart. She met his gaze, transfixed. "How does it work?"

"You have to accept it and then let it go. You can't keep going back to revisit the pain." He took a long drink to let that simple truth sink in.

Brie was moved by his words. "Yes, you're right..."

Faelan put his beer down and looked at them both. "I killed a boy. It was my fault. I can't change it. Mary helped me see that I had imprisoned myself in that guilt and grown used to the pain." He closed his eyes and groaned. "That was where my true weakness was, in allowing myself to accept the pain to the point where I refused to let go."

He opened those hypnotic blue eyes and stared into Brie's with a soulful gaze that took her breath away. "I will never be that weak again."

She ran a finger along the rim of her glass, at a loss for words. "That is profound, Mr. Wallace."

Faelan addressed Lea. "Who could have guessed that seeing Brie tied up while jogging on the beach would mark the beginning of my re-entry into humanity?"

Lea shrugged. "It's crazy, the turns life takes..."

"Now I am determined to help Mary face that same truth. She has to let go of the pain she clings to. She thinks of it as her shield against the world, but in reality it's killing her."

Brie suddenly understood how perfect Faelan was for Mary. Only someone who had suffered deeply would have the authority to bring her through it. "I'm grateful she found you, Mr. Wallace."

He ignored her compliment. "I need you to support Mary. Do not let her down."

"Of course," Brie answered easily.

But Faelan was quick to add, "Even when she bites back…and she will."

Both girls had suffered Mary's backlashes in the past, but Brie appreciated the reminder. She assured him, "Through thick and thin, Mr. Wallace."

He lifted his glass and clinked it against both of theirs. "Do not fail her."

Tono came to collect Lea for the scene they would be performing together. He glanced at Faelan and asked Brie, "Is everything fine here?"

Brie smiled to reassure him. "Couldn't be better."

Faelan stood up and handed Mary's purse to Brie. "No problems here, old man." He left them and moved over to a group of fawning submissives.

Lea grabbed Tono's arm and squeezed it. "Can't wait for tonight's scene!"

Tono put his hand lightly on Brie's shoulder. "You know where to find me, should you need anything."

"Yes, Tono. Thank you. I think I'll hang with Mary for a bit longer."

Lea turned to Brie as they were leaving and whispered, "He promised to spank me this scene!"

Brie had to admit she was jealous, especially when all she could do was observe other people all night. Several subs descended on Lea's seat and fought over it, filling the space instantly. Brie guarded Mary's stool fiercely until she finally showed up.

"What took so long, Blondie?"

"Hey, I can't help it if Doms keep stopping to talk to me. I'm not allowed to be rude to them, now, am I?" she said with a self-satisfied smirk.

"Whatever…"

"I'm telling you, Brie. You're missing out."

Brie didn't want another lecture about being collared, so she changed the subject. "So what are your plans tonight?"

Blonde Nemesis answered with a cocky tilt of her chin, "Wouldn't you like to know?"

"Why do you have to be such a pain?"

"Haven't you always touted that we should be true to our hearts? Well, I *truly* don't want to tell you, so suck on that."

Brie groaned. *Why do I even try?* She suddenly heard frantic whispering all around her.

Mary stood up and announced, "He's here." She moved forward, trying to get a better look at the man. Brie got up to follow her, but couldn't stay close because of the crush of females. She satisfied her curiosity by watching the tall, midnight-skinned African from afar.

He studied each sub as he made his way through the crowd, stopping at every alcove to take in the scene but moving on abruptly, obviously on the prowl.

Even Brie felt a sexual attraction as he approached. He caught her eye, glanced briefly at the collar around her neck and moved on without pausing.

She let her breath out once he'd passed by. To scene with a man as imposing as Master O would challenge any sub, but the fact his expertise involved blood took it to an entirely different level.

The Haven did not allow blood play on its premises. Whichever sub was chosen tonight would be required to leave with Master O. Although that was normally frowned upon by the club, the Dom's experience and reputation allowed him to circumvent standard protocol as long as he procured a willing sub—and there were *plenty* who were willing.

It did not come as a surprise to Brie when Master O eventually approached Mary. Brie could feel the collective tension of the subs around her. They deeply resented his choice.

"Your name?" he asked in a dark, velvety voice.

Mary looked up and smiled, obviously pleased she had been the one chosen. She answered demurely, "It's Mary, Master O."

"I would like to scene privately with you...Mary." His voice dropped to a low growl when he spoke her name. The timbre of his voice had even Brie quivering.

Mary batted her eyelashes at the Dom, before bowing low in respect. Brie knew what a cherished dream this was—to experience blood play performed by a famed master of the sport. That was why it came as a complete shock when Mary answered, "I am honored, Master O, but I fear I must decline tonight." She gave him a coy smile, one that invited the chase.

Brie heard a gasp from one of the other subs.

The Dom appeared equally stunned. He looked Mary up and down reproachfully. "Ah, my mistake. You are unworthy of such an invitation." He turned his back on her, and began studying a group of girls nearby. Eventually, he picked a curvaceous sub with platinum hair to accompany him out of the club.

After Master O had left, a band of spiteful subs encircled Mary.

Brie heard one hiss, "You don't belong here. You pretend to be a submissive, reeling them in with your looks, but you're really just a fucked-up piece of white trash. He figured it out quickly enough though, didn't he? They all do…"

Another echoed the sentiment, "Worthless piece of trash."

Mary held her head up higher, but said nothing. It distressed Brie that Blonde Nemesis wasn't lashing out.

The girl's lack of response sent a chill down Brie's spine because she knew what it meant. Their words were hitting close to home—tapping into Mary's greatest fear. Brie tried to push through the circle, desperate to grab onto Mary before she bolted from the club, but there was no need.

Faelan appeared beside Mary and barked, "Enough!" He placed his hand on the back of her neck and squeezed hard. Brie could see her visibly relax under his vise-like grip.

The Wolf's icy stare bored into the two girls who had dared to insult Mary. "This submissive is worth ten of you."

The wayward subs' haughty gazes instantly fell to the floor.

Faelan spoke loudly enough for everyone within earshot to hear his command. "From now on, you are not allowed to speak to Miss Wilson. You are unworthy of such an honor." He glanced at the other girls and added, "That will be true for the rest of you if you dare to speak disrespectfully to her. Do you understand?"

Brie knew that each girl in the group longed to partner with him. His displeasure was a true hardship for them. "Yes, Faelan," they answered.

He nodded curtly.

"It's time to serve," Faelan ordered, guiding Mary out of the circle of women and leading her to the empty alcove he had reserved. It was then that Brie understood why Mary had declined Master O. She was to be Falean's sub for the evening and had sacrificed her desires in order to honor her commitment.

Like a moth to a flame, Brie drifted to the scene, curious what Mary had requested. Tonight, as per his protocol, Faelan addressed the gathering crowd, informing them of his choice. "Miss Wilson has asked to play the reluctant spy." He smiled ominously. "Enjoy."

Brie struggled to breathe. This would be the same scene Mary had flipped out on during her first Auction Day with Tono. Brie understood that it was the embodiment of her father's abuse, which Mary was still fighting to overcome. After what had just happened with Master O, it seemed like such a scene was a train wreck waiting to happen—with an audience who might enjoy the carnage.

Mary's eyes watered as Faelan covered her head in a black hood and secured it. He guided her to a wooden chair and began to bind her to it.

Tears fell down Brie's cheeks as she imagined Mary

as a child, being bound by her father, apprehensive of the beating that was about to begin. Why did Blonde Nemesis insist on reliving her childhood over again?

Mary's words echoed in Brie's mind. *"I don't like pain, but I endure it. It's like I have a driving need to defeat it. Like…if I was able to bear it without fear, I would finally be the victor over him."*

There Mary was, once again, attempting to defeat her father even if it cost her sanity.

Please, Faelan, save Mary… Brie begged silently.

The Wolf became rough as he finished the last of the ties. Brie heard Mary whimper underneath the hood.

"Are you afraid?" he asked lustfully.

"No."

His chuckle was low and menacing. "Oh, but you will be…" Faelan circled around her slowly. He knew how to play the crowd as he simultaneously played with his subs. Everyone in attendance was in tune with the scene he was orchestrating.

Unexpectedly, he grabbed her blouse with both hands and ripped it open. Buttons flew haphazardly onto the floor. He left her chest exposed as he turned and rifled through his duffle bag.

Faelan approached Mary, carrying a large knife and wearing a dangerous grin. "I will tell you a little secret, spy. Even if you do everything I ask, I am still going to hurt you."

One of the subs near Brie sucked in her breath.

Even Brie felt the aggressive eroticism flowing from Faelan and her body responded, remembering her time alone with him—the chocolate, the dancing, the bruises…

He slid the edge of the blade under her bra and cut it with a quick motion, releasing her breasts from their restraint. "How does it feel knowing you are powerless to stop me?"

Mary growled with real anger, "You will not break me."

"I *will* break you." He pinched her nipple and rolled his fingers against it, causing her to cry out in pleasurable pain. "I guarantee it."

Faelan knelt beside her, grabbing her breast roughly. He took her nipple into his mouth and bit down, then he pull back cruelly with the sensitive flesh still clamped between his teeth. Brie gasped when he did it again to the other one. It looked incredibly painful, but Mary didn't make a sound.

He grazed the edge of the knife against her skin, starting at her stomach and dragging it slowly between her breasts, up to the hollow of her throat. Faelan pressed it against her pulsing skin, leaving an indentation without drawing blood.

"I know this is what you seek." He tossed the knife, and its clatter as it hit the floor filled the air. "Which is why I will not give it to you."

Mary growled in frustration and turned her head away from him. "Coward."

Faelan grasped her chin violently, pulling the hood off and hissing, "Worthless trash."

Brie whimpered. *No…* Mary could not handle Faelan turning on her too. It would be the end of her.

Mary's stubborn spirit could not be silenced. She

glared at the young Dom and challenged him, "Go on... Give me your worst."

He slapped her face, leaving a pink handprint on her cheek. "You will get exactly what you deserve."

Faelan put his hand under her skirt and forced his fingers between her closed legs. Mary gasped and then clamped her mouth shut, refusing to give him the satisfaction of her surrender.

"Are you ready to be broken?"

"Never."

"You *will* break," he taunted.

Mary stared him down, but flinched involuntarily when he raised his arm to backhand her. It was easy to tell that reality was blurring into her past. Brie could sense it, could feel the dangerous precipice Mary was teetering on.

Faelan swung, stopping an inch from her face. "No."

Mary's eyes popped open in surprise.

"Never again," he decreed. "You are not allowed to play out this scene. The past no longer has power over you." He bent down to whisper something into Mary's ear.

Her lips trembled slightly as she listened to Faelan. She stared ahead without speaking, his words seeming to have no effect until the tears began to flow. A heart-wrenching cry escaped Mary's lips.

Faelan pulled a small penknife from his pocket and swiftly cut her from her bonds, gathering Mary into his arms and holding her tightly as a flood of emotion tore at her. It was a terrible and powerful release that Mary couldn't control. Sheltering her, he picked her up and spirited her to one of the private rooms in the back of the club.

People stood gawking as they passed, wondering what had just happened. Brie pushed through them and began gathering Faelan's things. Her heart was racing as she picked up the large knife and the pieces of rope and stuffed them into the black bag.

Whatever Faelan had said must have affected Mary on a soul level. Brie had never seen the woman cry real tears—ever. She looked in the direction in which the two had disappeared. Tonight, the young Dom had broken the barrier no one else had. For the first time, Brie felt hope...for both of them.

Lea came running up just as Brie was sanitizing the area. "Oh-em-gee, Brie, what just happened? Everyone is talking!"

Brie smiled as she meticulously wiped down the chair. "Lea, I think Blonde Nemesis has found her Prince Charming. Faelan held the key to unlock her."

Lea shook her head in disbelief. "Someone actually got through to that woman? And it was the young pup, no less?"

"Mary caused quite a ruckus by rejecting Master O, but I'm so proud of her. She stayed true to her heart, despite the temptation the Master must have presented."

"Dang, girl—sounds like I missed *all* the action!"

Brie gave her an unsympathetic look. "Like I'm going to feel sorry for you, all tied up with Tono. But yes, it was amazing," she said wistfully. "So romantic, the way he stopped midway through backhanding her and said 'No'. But even more astonishing was seeing Mary really cry."

"Blonde Nemesis sobbing? I don't believe it."

Brie had seen the spark between them, and said with confidence, "Mark my words, Lea. I see a collaring in their future."

Lea's Erotic Surprise

The last day of production, Sir sent Brie an unusual text as they were wrapping up: *Go to the boutique next to the studio.*

With a little googling, Brie found the closest shop and headed there when she was done for the day. Even though it had been an exhausting week, she couldn't wait to discover what Sir had planned for the evening.

A little bell rang above the doorway, announcing her entrance into the boutique, but there wasn't a soul in the shop. She looked around and saw a gamut of sexy clothing, from catsuits and lingerie to full-length gowns.

"Hello?"

Brie moved up to the counter and saw a large box with a small envelope attached. Her name was on it. She took it off and read:

> Go to the flower shop by our apartment.
>
> Bring the box but do not open it.

Brie picked up the giant box, grinning as she

clutched it. What lay inside could be an evening gown, which meant a night out, or naughty lingerie for indoor play.

Clever Sir.

She texted him as soon as she was in the car. He responded with an extra assignment for her.

Put your feet on the dashboard on either side of the steering wheel.

Play with yourself until you're on the brink of orgasm.

Proceed to the flower shop.

Brie looked around at the busy sidewalk. She was nervous about masturbating in public, but did not want to fail Sir. She gingerly placed her high heels on either side of the wheel and scooted down a little so she wouldn't be as obvious.

Brie only received a few blank stares, so she reached between her legs and under her panties.

She suddenly understood the exhilaration of her assignment. Doing something wicked in broad daylight with the very real threat of detection was arousing in the extreme, which was also cruel, given the fact she wasn't supposed to orgasm.

Brie slipped her finger inside her pussy and coated it with her juices before pulling out and playing with her clit. It was already erect and sensitive. She swirled her finger over the responsive nub before giving it a good flicking.

Brie whimpered and had to stop. She was too turned

on to tease herself that way. Using two fingers, she slid in and out of her pussy, gliding her slick fingers over the folds of her outer lips, only brushing her clit lightly on occasion. Oh, yes, that felt good—like a relaxing back-rub for the loins.

But she knew that was not what Sir had asked of her. Brie returned to the quick flicking, seeing how long she could take it. Her pussy began to burn with need, demanding a quick release to end the torment. She was inclined to spoil it, but resisted the urge.

Just a little longer.

She made the mistake of looking up and meeting the gaze of a man walking past. The unexpected connection sent her over the edge. She squeaked, removing her fingers and scrambling to sit up, her pussy beginning to climax.

No, no, no…

Brie did the only thing she could think of to stop the tidal wave. She slapped her face hard. The pain brought her off the precipice and back down to earth. *Success!*

The man was still staring at her. Brie slipped her two fingers into her mouth, sucking off the remaining juices. "Yum," she mouthed before buckling up and starting the car.

She headed to the flower shop with a mischievous grin on her face. Sometimes it was wickedly fun to be bad.

Thank you, Sir.

Brie kept glancing at the box as she drove. Wrapped packages presented a terrible temptation. Sir knew the added torture he was putting Brie through by preventing her from taking a peek. He was probably at home, sipping a martini, amused by the thought of it.

Brie entered the tiny flower shop and went up to the girl at the counter, but was unsure what to say to her.

"Are you Miss Bennett?" the woman finally asked, after looking Brie over.

Brie smiled in relief. "I am, but how did you know?"

"I was told to look for a particular necklace."

Brie fingered her collar and smiled. "I *love* this necklace."

"It is quite lovely. I haven't seen one like it before," the shopkeeper replied. She handed Brie a single stem covered in a series of delicate orchids.

Brie took it and examined the blossoms, admiring the perfection of each individual flower. "This is stunning."

"Yes, it is. I was instructed to pick only the best for you."

Brie didn't see a card with further instructions, so she asked, "Is there anything else?"

"No, this is all."

Brie was slightly confused. Orchids reminded her of Tono, but that couldn't be right, so she texted Sir after leaving the shop. Unfortunately, she got no response. Was he up in the apartment, waiting for her?

She stared at the orchid again, remembering the haiku Tono had written. It had mentioned an erotic gift... But OMG—what if she was wrong and showed up at Tono's place uninvited? It would be all kinds of embarrassing.

Playing it safe, Brie made a quick stop by the apartment. She wasn't surprised to see it dark and silent. She checked every room just to be sure before getting into her car and heading to the Kinbaku master's place.

Now her imagination was running amok. Why would Sir have Brie spend time at Tono Nosaka's? She remembered he had mentioned that Lea's birthday gift was linked to Tono's.

Damn! Whatever they have planned is going to be freakin' amazing!

Brie pulled up to Tono's house and stared at it, feeling disappointed. His house was dark too. She got out of the car, assuming that Sir had left a card for her on the doorstep. However, as she approached she noticed a slight flickering through the window, as well as the hypnotic sound of a lone flute.

She knocked lightly, trembling all over as she waited for Tono to open the door. Instead, Lea graced the doorway dressed in a vibrant red kimono, her lips stylized in black to look like those of a geisha.

"Miss Bennett," she said in a formal voice, "please come in."

Brie stepped through the entrance with her large present, which Lea took from her before shutting the door.

The room was a fairyland of red candles.

"Lea, this is beautiful!"

"Kind of you to say, Miss Bennett," Lea said, trying to hide her grin. "I am here to clean and prepare you for the evening."

That sounded deliciously promising.

"Please follow me," Lea directed, leading Brie to Tono's bedroom.

Brie whispered, "What's going on?"

"I have waited months for this, Miss Bennett. I'm not about to spoil the surprise now," Lea informed her. "So be quiet and enjoy my preparations."

Brie giggled under her breath. The sexual tension flowing from Lea told her that this was going to be better than anything she had imagined. Brie just hoped the evening wouldn't end in a bad joke.

Lea undressed her slowly, laying her clothes on the bed. She then spent an hour cleaning her body, shaving her intimate parts and fixing her hair. All the months of stress slowly evaporated under Lea's gentle hands.

"I like the look of your brand," Lea purred, lightly tracing the mark. It ached at her touch, but Brie found it strangely erotic.

"Does it still hurt?" Lea asked.

"Not as bad as it did. To be honest, the branding itself didn't hurt nearly as much as the weeks after." Brie looked behind her, wishing she could see it. "Still, I love wearing his mark and I love looking at his."

"Sir has one too?"

Brie suddenly felt guilty, as if she had given away a privileged secret. "Forget I said anything. Please…"

Lea could tell she was upset and assured her, "Don't worry, Brie. I'm going to see it tonight anyway."

Brie gasped and turned to face her. "What?"

Lea cursed herself as she turned Brie back around. "Forget I said anything. Enough talk."

Lea giggled to herself as she continued her sensual preparations. When her friend had finished, she gave Brie a hug and a kiss on the cheek. "Now to unwrap your gift, birthday girl."

Brie tore into the package. Had it been anyone but Lea, she would have shown more decorum, but her best friend knew how wrapped gifts intrigued Brie. She lifted the lid and found a kimono that matched Lea's, but in black. It was covered in intricate embroidery. Brie realized on closer inspection that there were tiny orchids covering the silk. "This is unreal," she exclaimed, picking it up to put it on. She twirled around, feeling the cool silk flap lightly against her warm skin. She felt so wonderfully spoiled that she hugged herself.

"Miss Bennett, although it is beautiful on you, I need to complete your dress," Lea said, returning to her formal persona. She slid the garment off Brie's shoulders and laid it back on the bed.

Lea took a pair of stockings, garters and lacy crotch-less panties from the box. She helped Brie into them and then finished with the kimono, tying the sash tight around Brie's waist. Lea stood back and looked at her with the pride of a mother.

"Simply gorgeous, just as I envisioned." She dragged Brie to the mirror and they stood side by side. Lea had a red kimono and black lips, and Brie was her comple-ment, wearing a black kimono and red geisha lips.

"We make a beautiful pair," Brie said, laying her head on Lea's large chest.

"We always have," she replied, smiling at Brie in the mirror. "And now for your big surprise. I'm getting goosebumps just thinking about it."

Brie saw actual bumps on Lea's arm. "What are you planning to do to me?" she questioned, suddenly worried.

"Just you wait, Brie. I've watched you from the beginning of training. I know what you like. I think tonight will top everything. *Everything!*"

"Please—give me a hint, at least."

Lea led Brie out of the room. "You're just going to have to trust me."

Trust Lea?

Sir and Tono stood waiting for her. Both men were naked from the waist up, which was heavenly to behold. Sir was dressed only in black silk pants, and Tono in red.

Brie noticed two rings hanging from the ceiling above them. They were new, and gave Brie an inkling of what was in store.

"You look breathtaking, téa," Sir said, holding out his hand. Brie glided over to her Master on a cloud of wondrous expectation.

"Lea," Tono called. Lea walked over to stand beside the Asian Dom, her smile wide and beaming.

"So it's téa and Lea tonight, is it?" Brie commented.

"Yes," Tono replied smoothly. "It is not unusual for two girls to share an experience of Kinbaku."

Brie looked at Lea, barely able to contain her excitement. "Kinbaku *together?*"

Lea grinned. "Not exactly..."

Sir turned Brie's head and kissed her, sending little ripples of electricity through her already humming body. His low whisper sent chills through her. "Stand below the ring, hands behind your back, and wait."

She walked under it, looking up to make sure she was in the exact spot. Brie put her hands behind her back and smiled as Lea did the same, facing her, not more than two feet away.

Tono picked up a length of jute and unwound it. Just hearing it hit the floor made Brie's pussy wet. He came up behind Lea and secured the rope just under her breasts. Lea looked at Brie without speaking. The glint of lust in her eyes said it all.

Brie shivered when she felt Sir's lips next to her ear. "I want you to watch."

He kissed her neck, scratching her skin with his five o'clock shadow, as though he knew he was driving her crazy with the contact. Brie watched as Tono expertly wrapped Lea in jute, taking away her freedom to move, to breathe deeply. Her own body ached to feel the rope and she swayed slightly in need of it.

"Completely still, téa," Sir commanded as he knelt down. Brie cried out passionately when he bit her on the ass.

Lea gasped. "Oh, Brie. That little cry of yours turns me on."

Tono swiped his finger between Lea's legs and commented casually, "Yes, it does."

Brie bit her lip, liking this dynamic already.

Tono looped a length of the jute down between Lea's legs on one side of her outer lip and cinched it tight, and then he brought down another, leaving her pussy unobstructed for his pleasure. Brie did not miss the light touches he placed on Lea's mound as he worked, or the glazed look in Lea's eyes as she began to give in to the seduction of the rope.

He pulled at her kimono, uncovering Lea's impressive breasts in an artful manner. The way he exposed her was so sensual that Brie felt a gush of wetness. Watching her best friend enjoying Tono's expertise was intensely arousing.

Sir rubbed his middle finger against Brie's clit. It pulsed with desire. "No coming yet, téa. Not until your Master gives permission." He caressed her with more enthusiasm, making Brie whimper. She closed her eyes and laid her head back against his shoulder, trying to be good.

When she opened them again, she saw that Lea's hands were bound above her head, the rope anchored to the ring in the ceiling. Lea looked like a Japanese doll decorated in jute. "You're beautiful, Lea," Brie told her.

Lea smiled slowly, the rope already having its euphoric effect on her.

Brie's heart skipped a beat when she saw Tono approach *her* with a new length of jute. Sir left Brie's side, moving over to Lea. He opened a case and began laying out a series of attachments.

A violet wand…

Tono slipped the kimono off her shoulders, letting it drape over the sash. He then lifted her arms. Brie trembled, waiting for the first caress of the rope. As with Lea, he placed the first under her breasts. When he cinched it tight, she gasped involuntarily. It had been a while since her body had embraced the call of the jute.

"I feel your need," Tono stated quietly, as he slowly crisscrossed the rope to lift and separate her breasts. She sighed, loving the tight and pleasing constriction.

Tono bound Brie in a different pattern than Lea's,

leaving her back free of rope. As he worked, his hands teased but did not touch her mound. The spell of his seductive binding began to lift her soul. She let out a soft, contented moan. The slapping of the jute, the tugging, and the tight caress were sending her ever higher.

"Delicious, isn't it?" Lea whispered.

Brie nodded, not wanting to disturb the rush.

The buzz of the violet wand began, and Lea whimpered. Both girls were familiar with the distinctive sound. Brie opened her eyes and smiled at Lea. She was going to love Sir's electric touch.

Sir turned the device to medium, knowing Lea's affinity for it, and slowly moved the device up the inside of her leg. Lea started shaking as he got closer to her pussy. She stiffened and Brie could have sworn she orgasmed.

Brie cried out as she struggled to deny herself her own climax, and was surprised when no one reprimanded Lea for her lack of control. How was that fair?

Sir started up Lea's other leg, forcing Brie to take a deep breath. It was proving to be a challenging night. Again, Lea started shaking as Sir made his way up her inner thigh.

Fortunately, Tono distracted Brie, taking her wrists and quickly binding them together before looping the rope over the ring. As he pulled the jute taut, Brie was struck by a feeling of elegant femininity mixed with total helplessness.

"Ooh..." she moaned. She felt long and lean, with no ability to resist her Master's desires—the perfect combination.

Sir finished off his play with Lea by turning up the power and brushing her nipples. Lea screamed in surprise and then started giggling. It was so infectious that Brie couldn't help but giggle with her.

"Oh, Brie, that was good, so good…" she sighed when he was done.

Sir looked across at Brie and said, "And now it's your turn."

He carefully cleaned off the equipment and put it back in the case. Instead of bringing it with him, Sir walked over empty-handed, letting Brie know he had something else in mind for her.

Brie swayed in her bindings. There was no escaping whatever he planned to do. It was thrilling. Tono had done an excellent job of restraining her. She looked at Lea and mouthed the words, "Help me!"

Lea purred at her. "Never."

As Tono passed to return to Lea, he grazed his fingers lightly against Brie's nipple, sending tendrils of fire down to her groin.

Brie heard Sir unzip his bag, and then the distinctive thud as the end of the bullwhip hit the floor. Her body tingled all over. *Will he be gentle or rough?*

Lea's eyes lit up. Being so close to each other made it almost as if they were experiencing each action as one.

Tono's home was unique, with high ceilings. They were perfect for Kinbaku as well as accommodating a bullwhip. Brie heard Sir warming up as the end of the bullwhip snapped near her.

Brie found the whip challenging, like no other tool Sir used. It forced her to a level of submission she struggled to maintain. Her fear was real, but her trust absolute.

She was hyperventilating, but did not become aware of it until Tono spoke softly. "Breathe with me…"

His simple command was a welcomed reminder. She closed her eyes and listened for Tono's breath, which brought instant calm to her soul. She quickly became in sync with him and, with a stroke of genius, she told Lea, "Breathe with us."

The three became one as they took deep, soul-refreshing breaths.

Sir approached Brie and gently pushed her hair forward, exposing her back to him. "Are you ready, téa?"

"Yes, Master," she breathed out in a calm voice.

He stepped back and waited a few seconds, building the suspense.

She was actually relieved when she heard the rush of air as the whip came hurling towards her. Because of her heightened arousal, the light stroke sent a burst of sexual energy straight to her loins.

"Does it feel good?" Lea whispered.

Brie nodded.

"Yum…" her friend said, as if she could feel it.

The lick of the whip was stimulating and alluring. Just as Master Anderson had predicted, her pussy quivered with the knowledge Sir could deliver a fiery stroke…but he did not.

After several minutes of the sensual stimulation, he paused. "Now," he said ominously.

Brie felt the lash of the whip across her buttocks as she watched Tono smack Lea's ass. Both Brie and Lea cried out in unison. It was extremely erotic.

"Color, téa."

"Green, a brilliant green, Master," she answered, hoping he would do it again.

To Brie's delight, he cracked the whip across her ass repeatedly. The sharp burst of fire across her skin multiplied the burning in her groin. She enjoyed watching Lea receive her spanking, knowing her friend was feeling the sting of the whip vicariously.

It was incredibly sexy, but that darn Lea came again, right there in front of her. Brie had to close her eyes when Tono began playing with Lea's clit. Why were they being so cruel? Wasn't this supposed to be *her* birthday present, not Lea's?

Sir finished the session with several light licks, like tender kisses. It was a sweet ending with the bullwhip, something she hadn't experienced before. He came up behind her and whispered in her ear as he caressed her smarting ass.

"Watching you receive my strokes, the way your beautiful ass rolls with each contact of the whip, the way your muscles tense and release…it is arousing, babygirl."

She turned her head towards him. "Thank you, Master."

His tongue caressed the outside of her lips as his fingers reached between her legs and teased her wet opening.

Brie moaned, feeling her pussy tensing for an orgasm. She cried, "Red… Red!"

Sir chuckled. "Your orgasm will be grand, téa. When I allow it."

He pressed his finger inside and teased her G-spot, making her thighs shudder involuntarily. "Yes, an orgasm of epic proportions, but not yet."

Sir nodded to Tono and both men began loosening the bindings. Brie watched as Tono made quick work of the knots and the jute fell from Lea. He then untied the sash and lifted the kimono from her shoulders, laying all three items on the mat.

The knots proved more challenging for Sir, but soon she felt the jute's release. The feeling of lightness it gave her was almost like a spiritual liberation. Looking at Lea's body covered in beautiful rope marks brought a smile to Brie's lips. She knew she carried the same lovely marks— a charming gift left by the jute for their Doms to admire.

Her skin tingled where the jute had been, extending the delicious experience.

Sir loosened the sash, letting the kimono fall to the floor. She stood before him, naked except for the hose, garters, and panties—his favorite look for her.

He ran his fingers over the indentations of the rope, sending chills through her. "Exquisite."

To Brie's surprise, Sir bent down and picked up one of the lengths of jute, then began binding her wrists again. Tono did the same, looping the end through the ring and forcing Lea's arms back up.

Brie bit her lip as Sir tightened the rope again, binding her arms tightly. What were they going to do now?

"Bend forward at the waist, both of you," Sir ordered.

The girls did, facing each other, now only a foot apart. With careful precision, the Doms released the tautness of the ropes until Brie's and Lea's noses were only inches from each other. Lea smiled at her and leaned forward, giving her a quick kiss on the lips. Both girls giggled.

"A little tighter," Tono suggested.

The two were pulled back just a fraction, so no contact could be made. When the adjustments were complete, they were tightly secured to the rings again.

Curiosity was killing Brie. "What are you doing, Master?"

Sir glanced at her and winked before addressing Tono. "I think they need to be silenced." He pulled a gag from his pocket and commanded, "Open." When Brie parted her lips, smooth silk instantly filled the gap. Sir tied it firmly and then stood back.

Instead of silk, Tono wrapped several strands of jute around Lea's mouth to act as her gag. Lea looked at her and wiggled her eyebrows, as if to say, *Aren't we naughty girls?*

"The time has come, téa."

She held her breath, hoping her ecstasy would be close at hand.

Sir instructed, "I want you to keep your eyes locked on Lea—do not let them stray. I am going to fuck you hard. I will be rough."

She whimpered, very much liking the sound of that.

"You are free to orgasm as many times as you want, as long as you continue to look into your friend's eyes. I want her to be able to count the number of your pleasures."

Naked and bound, Brie met Lea's gaze and thought,

Oh, this is going to be hot on a whole new level…

Sir undressed behind her as Tono removed his clothing in front of her. She admired the Asian Dom's toned body, a perfect male specimen according to her own specifications. And now she was going to watch him in action—with her best friend, no less. It was all kinds of erotic!

Tono looked up with those chocolate-brown eyes and she suddenly felt like a deer in headlights, caught by their connection. Her heartbeat increased as both men took their positions. It was almost like watching a mirror as she felt Sir's hands on her waist and saw Tono grab onto Lea's hips.

Brie lowered her gaze and stared at Lea. This was it—they were going to be pounded at the same time, by two gorgeous Doms, while facing each other.

It's good to be me…

Sir forced Brie to arch her back more, and then penetrated her slowly until he found an angle he liked. He traced her brand with his finger, causing her pussy to contract around his cock. "No mercy for my goddess."

Sir grunted as he rammed his cock deep inside, the head of his shaft rubbing hard against her swollen G-spot. Brie screamed into her gag while her body invited the ferocity of it—*needed* it, in fact.

Lea's eyes widened as Tono began his own thrusting. Lea's breasts bounced crazily as he pounded with fervor. Neither Dom was taking it easy tonight.

Brie screamed into the gag again as the crest she had been teetering on for hours completely overwhelmed her and she experienced what she could only describe as a full-body orgasm. Every part of her seemed to tense almost to breaking point, and then explode in orgasmic release—from the tips of her toes up the entire length of her spine, to the individual hairs on her head.

Tears fell freely as she rode the intense tidal wave of pleasure.

Lea's face had screwed up in her own orgasm, but Brie's lasted far longer—far, far longer.

Sir finally pulled out and instructed her to breathe in deeply. She heard him coating his shaft in lubricant. It could only mean one thing...

Brie almost shut her eyes in pleasure when she felt him press against her sphincter, but Sir had given her specific instructions. She opened them and concentrated on Lea's pupils as he eased his hard shaft into her ass. Sir gave sexy, stinging slaps on her ass cheeks as he forced himself in deeper.

Just as he had before, Sir thrust leisurely until he found the perfect spot. He chuckled when he finally found it.

Brie tensed, but he murmured, "Relax, babygirl, relax..." He turned her head to kiss her. Once she had surrendered to him, his lips were fierce and demanding.

Sir grabbed a fistful of her hair, pulling her head back as he began thrusting into her with powerful strokes, over and over again. Reality blurred as primal sensations took hold. His cock was hitting her G-spot, but from a different angle, causing a different reaction. As soon as he stopped, her pussy caught up, gushing with liquid as it clamped down in a rhythmic dance.

Brie stared at Lea, but struggled to focus. As soon as

the last contraction had ended, Sir started up again. It didn't take long for her body to respond with another, equally powerful orgasm.

Brie shook her head in disbelief. She knew her body well. Normally, with each consecutive orgasm the intensity and pleasure decreased, but not this time. She looked at Lea in wonder as Sir began again. There was no question he was going to make her gush for him a third time.

He started pounding again, and had no problem bringing her to that point almost immediately. She whimpered as another orgasm rocked her body and her pussy released a smaller ejaculation than before.

"We're getting close," he growled.

Close to what?

Sir began playing with her clit as he slowly caressed her ass with his shaft. It was too much, and she stiffened in a long, drawn-out orgasm.

Help me… Brie pleaded silently to her friend.

Sir commanded, "Come for me, téa."

At only the lightest pressure on her clit, with his cock filling her ass, Brie came for him again.

"Again."

Brie shook her head in astonishment as her pussy orgasmed on command, stealing her conscious thought with its intensity. Subspace called and she entered willingly, letting the tingly feeling take over while her body continued to listen and respond to Sir. Pure bliss and a level of heightened serenity carried Brie deeper within as Sir pounded into her again.

Everything fell away as she *became* sensation and

found a whole new world to explore…"

"Téa…"

A light tapping on her cheek caught her attention, and she listened more carefully.

"Téa… Open your eyes."

They fluttered open of their own accord, and she gazed into the loving eyes of her Master. She tried to smile, but her muscles were too relaxed to respond.

Sir leaned over and kissed her. "I sometimes wonder just how far you fly from me, babygirl."

She struggled to turn her head and saw they were lying on Tono's floor mat. The candles had been blown out, and the room was dark except for a single tealight.

"Sir," she croaked.

He put his finger against her lips. "No need to talk. Now that I have you back, we can go home."

Home.

When Sir picked her up, she realized she had been wrapped back into the smooth silk of her black kimono. She laid her head against his chest and smiled.

"Did you enjoy yourself?"

She nodded.

"How were your climaxes?"

She was silent for a few moments, trying to find the word she wanted to share. "Legendary."

...On the Way to the Theater

The night she had been waiting for all her life had finally come—the premiere of her first film, her *baby*. A film she hoped would change the world in some small, but positive way.

People were going to see more than just a simple documentary. The film revealed Brie's personal transformation from the shell of a girl she had been into the fully actualized woman she was now. Would people recognize the significant, soul-level change or only see the kink? As Sir zipped up the back of her blood red gown, Brie suddenly felt a twinge of fear.

"What's wrong, téa?"

She turned around with tears in her eyes. "What if they don't understand? What if they don't get it, Sir?"

"It's the risk you take. You cannot force people to see what you see. All you can do is present your truth to them."

She swallowed hard. "For the first time, Sir..." Brie gazed into his confident eyes, "I'm scared."

He smiled as he put his hand under her chin and tilted her head higher. "Why did you make this film?"

"To share a new world of desires and a level of satisfaction people might not know exists."

"Do you feel your documentary accomplishes that?"

She gave a half-smile, understanding where he was heading with the question. "Yes, Sir, I do."

"Then whatever happens tonight, it will have gone well enough, agreed?"

Brie pressed her forehead into his chest. "Well enough…" she echoed. "But if it were up to me, I would prefer 'well enough' to mean a huge success, with lots of positive press and millions of enthusiastic fans."

Lifting her chin again, he asked in a serious tone, "Is that why you did it?" His intense gaze pierced her soul and the arrow of truth flew straight into her heart.

"No, Sir."

"Do not waste your energies on the unimportant."

She tiptoed to kiss Sir's firm lips. "As always, you give me the perspective I need. Thank you, Sir."

"This journey we embark on tonight will be a challenge, I'm certain of it. But I said it once and I will say it again, so that we are clear. No matter how this affects our lives, I'm proud to stand with you in this moment."

A lone tear escaped Brie's eye and rolled down her perfectly made-up face. Sir brushed it away with his thumb. "Exude elegance and poise, confident in the knowledge you are mine, Brie."

She smiled, remembering he had said those words the night of her collaring.

He returned her smile and announced, "I have a surprise for you."

She was grateful for any distraction, thinking he'd gotten her flowers or jewelry. "What is it, Sir?"

"Your parents are joining us tonight. They're on their way here as we speak."

She swallowed hard, trying to keep the shock from her face. "My parents?"

"I asked them to come and support you tonight."

"And my dad agreed?" Brie asked, unable to believe it.

He nodded as he turned her back around and placed a delicate chain around her neck. "They may not care for the path you have chosen, but their love for you remains constant."

She touched the necklace, noticing that it fit right under the collar she wore as if it were a part of it. "What's this?"

"A little reminder," he said, kissing the nape of her neck.

Brie walked over to the wall mirror to look at it. The intricate piece rested on her collarbone. She leaned closer to see the silhouette of two condors in flight, their wings outstretched and touching, connected to one another.

She was in awe. "Where did you find this?"

"I had it made for you."

"It matches the collar so perfectly, Sir. I..." She turned to face him. "There will never be a more perfect gift." Brie glanced in the mirror again, smiling as she touched the condors. She believed the necklace held the same significance as a wedding band.

She put her hands on Sir's chest and gazed up at him. "I love you, Thane Davis." Her insides fluttered as she said his given name.

He leaned down and kissed her. "I love you too, Brie Bennett, with all the fierceness of a condor."

She could feel the light pressure of the birds on her neck when she kissed him back. Whatever happened, nothing could touch her. She was protected by Sir's love.

The ride in the limo was miserably silent. Despite the fact that her parents had come to support Brie, it was obvious they hadn't changed their minds about Sir or the BDSM lifestyle. She could feel the judgment rolling off her father in waves. He refused to acknowledge Sir and it mortified Brie.

She looked around the spacious limousine and shuddered. Nothing good ever came out of a limo ride.

Sir had insisted they act vanilla in front of her parents. It made for a strained and difficult trip. Brie was nervous about the premiere, so she placed her hand on Sir's thigh for comfort, although she would have preferred to be at his feet.

Brie tried to kill the deafening silence by forcing a conversation. "So Mom, did you watch my film?"

Her mother gave her father an uneasy glance before answering. "I did…"

"And what did you think?"

"Frankly, I found it shocking."

"Is that all?" Brie asked, leaning forward, hoping to hear something positive from her lips.

"I like your friend Lea."

Brie sat back, disappointed that was all her mother had to say. She looked out of the window and said, "Yes, Lea is a funny girl."

"Will all the men who used you be there?" her father asked coldly.

She turned towards him, looking her father directly in the eye. "The men who helped train and support me will be there. If you have nothing nice to say to them, say nothing at all. They do *not* deserve your contempt."

"That is my intention, daughter. I will remain silent," he replied, glancing at Sir briefly to emphasize his meaning.

Brie groaned inside. "Why did you come tonight, Dad? If all you're going to do is make me feel bad and insult the man I love by ignoring him, what's the point? You might as well have stayed home."

"I came, daughter, because the man beside you insisted I was needed tonight. It seems obvious to us both that he was mistaken."

"That's not true! I'm glad Mr. Davis invited us," Brie's mother exclaimed, clutching her husband's hand. She smiled at her daughter. "Sweetie, even though this is not the kind of premiere I ever dreamed I would be attending, I *want* to be here. You are everything to me."

"Will you both stay to watch the film?" Brie pressed.

Her father growled. "Do you realize the sacrifice this is going to be for me as your father?" He stared at Brie harshly. "Do you?"

"No, Father. I can't imagine," she answered simply, biting back an ugly retort.

"I am going to be exposed to things a father should never have to witness. On top of that, I get to live with the knowledge that the rest of the world has seen it too. You are *my* daughter, *my* little girl."

"I am the girl you raised to be an independent adult. If my happiness is important to you, then you no longer need to worry. I am not only happy, but content and successful. I am living my dream."

"And my nightmare," he mumbled under his breath.

"You know, Dad, I'm glad you're going to watch my documentary. At least you won't be able to make ignorant statements anymore."

"We're about to pull up," the limo driver interrupted.

Brie looked out at the crazy amount of people crowding around the theater. "I never expected such a turnout for a documentary film," she said in wonder. She was thrilled until she saw the protest signs.

Oh, no…

Sir saw them too. "Head up at all times, Brie. You are focused on me. No one else matters."

She remembered a similar lesson in Russia. She closed her eyes and repeated to herself, *No one else matters.* When she opened her eyes, Brie felt a new sense of calm.

She told her parents, "Follow us, but *please* don't speak to anyone. These people don't need extra cannon fodder to use against me or my film."

"Our lips are sealed," her father replied, his expression hard and unwavering.

Her mother looked at the angry multitudes milling outside the car and panicked. "Brie, I don't want them to hurt you!"

Sir assured her, "She'll be fine, Mrs. Bennett."

Sir then cradled Brie's face in his hands and smiled. "Your moment has finally come, Brie. Embrace it with pride and confidence." He kissed her deeply, right there in front of her father. The boldness of the gesture infused her with a rebellious self-confidence.

When the driver opened the door for them, angry shouts filled the vehicle. Sir made her parents go first. "Wait beside the car, and then follow behind us."

Sir exited next. He stood up outside the limo and held his hand out to her. Brie took it and squeezed it hard, needing his courage.

"Slut!" was the first word to greet Brie as she emerged from the limo. She looked at Sir and smiled. If that was the best they could do, this was going to be easy.

She was enamored by the red carpet at her feet and the velvet ropes sectioning off each side. Hundreds of flashes went off as Sir held out his arm to escort her down the carpet.

Brie looked into the barrage of flashing lights and saw news cameras as well. Brie assumed the coverage would be a good thing, whether it was for the documentary or the protesters.

She was surprised to see Master Anderson standing just inside the ropes, and farther down, Master Coen as well. She wondered if they'd been asked to walk the red carpet as well, since both were mentioned in the film.

"Miss Bennett!" one of the reporters called out.

Sir led Brie over to the woman. She smiled at the reporter as she nervously played with the condors around her neck.

"Can you tell us why you created this documentary?"

"Certainly. I wanted people like me to have a better understanding of the D/s lifestyle." She giggled. "To be honest, when I first learned about it I was pretty shocked. But through my training, I've come to understand the beauty and power that can come from it."

"Beauty—I'll say! Just look at these hunky men you worked with," the reporter said, giving Sir a flirtatious wink.

Brie ignored her remark, and leaned towards the microphone. "I hope my documentary can open people's minds and bring couples closer together."

The reporter continued to flirt with him. "Closer is exactly where I'd like to be."

Sir frowned and moved Brie on to the next reporter in line. He leaned down and whispered, "Well done. Keep it about the film."

The male reporter she approached looked to be as old as her parents. Brie was already dreading his questions.

"Miss Bennett, this documentary is based on your own training. Is that correct?"

"Yes, it documents the six-week training I experienced at the Center."

"Did you go into training with the intention of documenting it, or was submission something you wanted to become skilled at?"

"Great question!" she complimented, realizing she had a true reporter on her hands. "I joined the Center because I was curious about the lifestyle after receiving an invitation from the headmaster of the school."

"When you say 'headmaster', you are speaking about the man standing beside you, Sir Thane Davis, and not the current headmaster of the school?"

It appeared that the man had done his homework. "That's correct. Because I studied film, it only seemed natural for me to document my days as I lived them. After I got to know the other students, I asked them to add their experiences as well."

"Would you say you are close to your fellow classmates?"

Brie looked farther down the red carpet and saw that both Mary and Lea were ahead of her, answering questions under the protection of Faelan and Tono.

She glanced back at the reporter. "Yes, I'm most definitely close to both. Although Mary and I have our differences, as you will see in the film, both ladies are exceptional friends."

He surprised her with his next question. "Miss Bennett, do you feel this documentary may end up hurting the BDSM community in any way?" he asked.

It was a sobering thought. Brie frowned when she answered, "I certainly hope not. It's my belief that knowledge is power. How can learning about something new and dispelling preconceived ideas be a bad thing?"

"We need to move on, Brie," Sir informed her, guiding her forward.

The next young woman in line looked so eager to interview Brie that she wondered if the girl might secretly desire to become a submissive herself.

With a wide, virtuous smile, the reporter asked,

"Miss Bennett, are you concerned at all about the negative message this film will give to millions of women?"

Brie was taken aback. "What do you mean?"

"Violence against women. The utter contempt of social standards. Girls whoring themselves out to the highest bidder. Women allowing themselves to be treated like sex objects, or worse—animals. Is that really the message you want to send out to impressionable young ladies?"

"What you are talking about are the preconceived notions I hope to dispel with this documentar—" Brie stopped midsentence. She found herself staring into the eyes of Sir's mother, who was standing directly behind the reporter. Ruth wore a malicious grin on her perfect face.

From within the crowd a woman emerged, shouting, "Fucking whore!" The stranger threw something at Brie's face.

It crashed into Brie's skull when she tried to duck, the impact hard and painful. Sir immediately moved between her and the attacker, using his body to protect her as several people rushed up, pelting them with what she thought were rocks and shouting hateful words.

Time slowed down to a crawl for Brie. All the shouting and commotion became silent in the chaos. She glanced over and saw her father shouting angrily, but her mother stood frozen in place with a look of sheer panic.

Then Brie felt the ooze of blood from her forehead and down her cheek. She felt for the wound and was confused when she looked at her hand and saw yellow instead of red. A piece of eggshell that had been stuck to her hair fell to the crimson carpet at her feet.

Brie felt the sting of humiliation. Rocks would have been preferable.

Sir tightened his grip on her. "It's going to be all right. Marquis Gray is taking care of it."

She looked up and saw that a small army of staff members from the Training Center had descended upon the attackers and were 'escorting' them to police waiting nearby.

Now that the initial shock had passed, Brie was crushed by a wave of shame. She had just been egged in public and her beautiful dress was ruined. To make her humiliation complete, she heard the sound of hundreds of camera clicks. Brie pulled against Sir in the direction of the limousine, wanting to escape.

"No, babygirl," he said firmly.

She looked up at her Master—her hair matted with yolk, the tears ready to fall.

Sir pulled the decorative handkerchief from his pocket and smiled charmingly as he cleaned the egg from her face. He did it with such tenderness that Brie momentarily forgot the world.

After he was satisfied, he stuffed the dirty handkerchief back in his pocket and lifted her chin to kiss her. The kiss infused her with courage, reminding her that nothing else mattered.

Brie whispered when he let go, "Only you, Sir."

He nodded and held out his arm for her. She took a deep breath before holding up her head and smiling at the cameras.

Brie's mother came up and blurted out, "Wait just a second." She licked her fingers before rubbing them against Brie's temple. It was an action that Brie had hated as a child—mother-spit used to clean her face—but tonight it took on emotional significance.

Her mother stood back and looked her over. "Yes, all better."

"Thank you, Mom," Brie whispered.

She gave Brie a tight squeeze before stepping back to stand with her father.

Brie looked back and saw her dad nonchalantly brushing eggshell off Sir's shoulder. It was a simple gesture, but one that meant the world to Brie. It was the first sign of acceptance.

She mouthed the words, "Thanks, Dad."

He gave her a brief smile and then wrapped his arm around her mother's waist. "Shall we?"

They avoided the rest of the reporters, making their way directly into the theater. Brie could only imagine what the headlines would read in the morning.

"Why don't we both freshen up, Brie?" Sir said. "Your father can wait here for you, should you have need."

Brie liked the protective sound of that. She kissed her dad on the cheek before following her mom into the restroom. Although she had a dress polka-dotted with wet spots, Brie looked and felt tons better when her mother had finished cleaning her off.

Sir was standing beside her father, already waiting for her when the two emerged from the restroom.

"Beautiful," he complimented, kissing the back of

Brie's hand tenderly.

"Well done, Marcy," her father praised after looking Brie over. "It appears we were needed tonight, after all."

Their small party was led to the reserved area, where she was greeted by Mr. Holloway, Lea and Mary. Lea rushed up to Brie, wanting to dish about what had happened outside, but Sir shook his head. "Tonight is about celebrating Brie's achievement, Ms. Taylor."

Lea reluctantly sat back down. "Can I at least tell a joke?"

Sir and Brie both answered, "No!"

Lea huffed and slouched in her seat. Tono gave her a gentle nudge.

She immediately sat up, her blooming blush coloring her ample chest a bright shade of red. "I'm sorry," she whispered to Tono, loud enough for others to hear as the lights began to dim.

It made Brie giggle. Even without her jokes, Lea was good for a laugh.

Brie eagerly watched the audience and listened for their collective responses once the film started. She loved every giggle and chortle, but cherished even more the lustful gasps when Marquis and Lea filled the screen. She noticed several audience members swiping at their eyes when Mary confessed her feelings of brokenness. To Brie's delight, as the credits rolled, the entire theater broke out in applause.

When the lights came back up, both Brie and Mr. Holloway were asked to stand and take a bow together. The theater roared with a second round of applause as people gave them a standing ovation.

Brie felt embarrassed by the focused attention and tried to sit back down, but Sir would not allow it. "This applause is for you. Accept it gracefully, Brie."

She faced the audience again and smiled, but she knew the applause was for everyone involved in the film, not just her. Brie gestured for Lea and Mary to stand with her. Mr. Holloway did the same with the film crew. It felt right, all of them standing together as one.

Finally, she convinced Sir to stand up beside her. Brie laid her head against his shoulder with a smile so wide it hurt and a heart that was completely and utterly content.

The Aftershock

Brie's parents left later that evening. Her father said it was imperative they control the damage the film would cause in their close-knit community. Brie didn't mind. Her father had watched the film and had not spoken of it since. She figured he needed time to process it. So she spent a restless night in Sir's arms, worrying what the newspapers would say in the morning.

What she woke up to both astonished and pleased her. The front page of the *LA Times* read 'The Strength of a Dominant' and had a picture of Sir thoughtfully cleaning Brie's face after the attack. The same picture was plastered on the national news that morning. Instead of focusing on the film or even the protestors, all the news centered on was the unusual relationship between Sir and Brie.

Brie found out from the morning show that Sir now had a following of female fans, from young girls to grandmothers. Twitter was going crazy speculating about him and Facebook pages had been set up in his honor. Everyone wanted to know more about the man who'd defended Brie so gallantly.

Overnight, D/s went from being an obscure term used by kinky deviants to being something sweet and romantic. The morning news had 'experts' answering questions and a psychologist explaining in clinical terms the reasons why they thought people practiced BDSM. It was quite amusing, if not a little insulting.

Sir turned off the TV and folded the paper before putting it in the trash. "The firestorm has begun." Brie looked at the trash can, deciding to ask Lea later to save her a copy as a memento.

Brie smiled as she crawled onto the lap Sir offered. "Well, at least people are talking about it, Sir."

"I, for one, do not care to see my face everywhere."

Brie brushed her fingers over his jawline, which was rough with morning stubble. "But it's such a handsome face, Sir. I don't mind one bit."

He huffed in irritation. "It has serious repercussions, Brie. I doubt I will be taken seriously in the business world now."

Brie frowned, suddenly feeling nauseous. "I never considered that, Sir."

Sir chuckled at her statement. "Why am I not surprised?" He pulled her head back and gently kissed her throat before biting it. His lips moved up to her ear. "I understood the consequences, but never considered they would belittle my lifestyle in this way." He shook his head in disgust. "Facebook pages?"

"It's kind of sweet, Sir," Brie told him, kissing his chin.

"What it does is diminish my authority, Brie. We are

not a sideshow to be gawked at and thereby dismissed."

She finally understood the gravity of the situation. "What do you suggest I do, Sir?"

"Only respond to serious inquiries and ignore frivolous issues meant to distract. Your duty is more than simply garnering press for the documentary—it is also about being respectful to the community we are a part of. Whether or not Mr. Holloway agrees, I believe that takes precedence over the film."

She understood his point and acquiesced. "I will do as you suggest, Sir."

The positive attention they had enjoyed quickly turned dark when rumors spread that Sir had abandoned his dying mother. As quickly as people had embraced him, they turned and crucified him.

'Woman-hater' became Sir's new title in the press. Clients he had worked with for years ended their association within hours of the accusations being released. The financial impact was terrible and swift.

Ruth had done her job well. She'd accomplished exactly what she'd promised. It broke Brie's heart to see his reputation decimated, but Sir seemed unruffled. In fact, he smiled when she asked why he was so calm.

"This is a litmus test, Brie. Any client who would react to such a rumor is not worth my time."

The next morning, everything changed yet again. Brie was watching the news with Lea and Mary. It amazed the girls how fickle the public could be and Lea was about to make a joke when Brie heard, "Next up, how you can help support Ruth Davis in her fight against cancer."

Brie called Sir immediately.

His answer surprised her. "Good. It's time the beast was flayed."

The girls continued to watch the television and were soon rewarded with a newsflash. Under Sir's orders, his lawyer had sent evidence of her falsified medical history to the major media outlets. It didn't take long before the news that Ruth Davis was cancer-free spread like wildfire and all donations were halted.

Reporters then set out to discover the *real* story behind Ruth Davis and left no stone unturned in their pursuit. Within days, the murky state of her financial affairs came to light, as well as issues in her past—including her infidelity and the death of her husband, Alonzo Davis.

The negative press quickly transferred from Sir to Ruth and, in the aftermath, droves of women naïvely flocked to the documentary to find out more about the tragic hero they knew as Sir Thane Davis.

What they found instead was the power of submission.

Farewell and Good Riddance

B rie was on her knees, back straight, breasts out, her hands behind her back. The clock was ticking in the kitchen, marking each second until Master's return.

She was startled by heavy pounding at the door. Brie cautiously approached it and peeked through the peephole, terrified it might be Sir's mother.

She was shocked to find it was Ms. Clark.

"Open up! Open up now—I demand to have answers!"

Brie ran down the hallway and threw on a summer dress before returning to the door. "Sir's not here, Ms. Clark, but I expect him in a few minutes."

Ms. Clark answered in a condescending tone, "Then let me in to wait for him."

"I have to get permission first," Brie called through the door. She texted Sir and was told to let the fuming Domme in.

Brie unlocked the door, quelling her unease as she allowed Ms. Clark to enter. Her ex-trainer brushed past her as if she didn't exist and headed straight for the couch. When Brie asked if there was anything she needed, Ms. Clark held up her hand and barked, "Do *not* speak to me."

Brie backed away slowly and returned to the door to kneel in the proper position until Sir's return.

The clock ticked loudly in the kitchen as the two waited. It was an unbearable silence, at least for Brie. Ms. Clark's anger was palpable and her contempt for Brie equally apparent. So she closed her eyes and entertained happy thoughts of being tied down by Sir, and of being tortured by his cock.

"Get that smirk off your face," Ms. Clark snapped.

Brie instantly frowned for the Domme's benefit, but in her head she begged, *Hurry home, Sir!*

Relief came when she heard his keys in the door. Sir dropped them on the counter and patted her head as he passed, letting her know she could stand up and join him.

"What are you doing here, Samantha?"

"Why? Why, Thane? Why do you hate me?"

"Calm down and explain," he ordered. "I have no clue what you're talking about."

"Tell your sub to leave," Ms. Clark demanded.

"No."

Ms. Clark looked first shocked and then dismayed. In a subtle act of defiance, she turned her back on Brie before explaining, "You told them to let me go and now I'm no longer working for the Center."

"Ah…" Sir took off his jacket and hung it up before joining her on the couch. "That had nothing to do with me, Samantha. That was your own fault."

"What the hell do you mean?" Ms. Clark demanded.

"Did you really think your stunt at Brie's party would have no consequences? All of the trainers were there, including the headmaster. With that one action, you demonstrated your utter lack of control. We'd seen it before with Brie, but unfortunately you never recovered, even after she'd left. The trainers must have decided it was time to give you the freedom you need to overcome that weakness."

"But you *know* I am a damn good trainer. How could you let them do this to me?!"

"I was not involved. But truthfully, I am in agreement with their decision. You need to move forward. It is time you break from the past that has held you down."

"What are you saying?" she said, her voice trembling as if she was about to cry.

"You have stuck by my side all these years with the mistaken hope that one day Durov would change his mind. I am telling you now—that will never happen."

"But... I don't believe it. Rytsar didn't press charges that night. I know he did that for me. He cared enough to protect me, despite everything. It was a horrible mistake and I've done my penance with unfailing determination. I've been waiting patiently all these years for his forgiveness. I've learned my lesson and am ready for him to grant it."

Sir shook his head. "Samantha, you are gravely mistaken. The reason he didn't press charges had nothing to do with protecting you. What you did to him was so degrading he could not stomach bringing it before a judge. To this day, you've never owned up to the damage you caused him."

"That's not true! I went to counseling; I quit drinking. Hell, I even became a submissive to another woman for him. Everything I did, *everything*, has been for him."

Sir's voice was harsh when he replied, "Everything you did has been for you, and you alone. You wanted him back, so you did those things in the hope that he would return to you. It's never been about him."

Ms. Clark glared at Sir, as if she hated his version of the truth.

He continued, indifferent to her wrath, "Samantha, it's possible to make a mistake so great you can never know closure with the person you have wronged. You can't undo the damage and you can't change the past. It's time to move on."

"But…" Her voice dropped down to a whisper. "Oh, God… "A tear fell down her cheek when she confessed, "I still love him."

Sir's response was stern but clear. "If you love him, you will move on."

Ms. Clark slumped on the couch, sounding hollow and weak when she asked, "How can I face a future without him?"

"Durov was never a part of your future."

It seemed surreal to Brie when Ms. Clark moved over and laid her head on Sir's shoulder. It was weird to see the woman underneath that hard exterior—like seeing a turtle without its shell.

Sir was gentle with her. He put his arm around Ms. Clark, saying, "You are an exceptional trainer and a skilled Mistress. There is no reason not to move forward with confidence. Claim the life you have put on hold."

She mumbled into his shoulder, "But the Center *was* my life."

"I understand, but trust me when I say you'll get used to it. It's a hard adjustment in the beginning. However, other things will take its place. My advice? If it gets to be too much, you can always visit. I know it's helped me."

Ms. Clark sat still in his arms for a few moments longer before sitting up and moving away from him, her hard persona back in place. "So that's it then. My time at the Training Center is officially over." She stood up and walked over to the window. "I have never felt so out of control of my own life before," she said as she gazed at the city below.

"That is only an illusion, Samantha. You were never in control, not until this very moment."

The Domme gasped. She closed her eyes and let it sink in. When she finally turned to face Sir, she stated, "I will miss your wisdom, Sir Davis." She glanced at Brie and her eyes narrowed briefly.

She focused her attention back on Sir. "Master Anderson is planning to move back to Colorado to start up a Training Center there. He's invited me to join him, along with Baron."

Sir put his hands behind his head and sat back on the couch, looking a bit stunned. "I'd actually forgotten that was Brad's original plan."

Brie wondered what Sir was thinking. Was he sad to lose his friend?

The stunned look was replaced with cool assurance.

He stood up, telling her, "This will be a good opportunity for the three of you. I'm confident you will work well as a team."

Ms. Clark shook Sir's hand, stating in a businesslike manner, "It's been a good run, Sir Davis." She paused. Her voice was thick with emotion when she spoke again. "I will never forget your support these many years." She bowed her head. "Thank you."

He placed his hand on the top of her head in a silent exchange. When he removed it, the Domme looked up and smiled sadly. Then she turned and stared hard at Brie.

"I have always found you irritating and disrespectful. Why do you think that is, Miss Bennett? I have yet to put my finger on it."

Brie blanched at her blunt words and sputtered, "Maybe…maybe I'm too much like you?"

The Domme scoffed, "No. You couldn't be more my opposite." Ms. Clark walked up to her, invading her personal space to stare at Brie's mouth. The ex-trainer's proximity was unsettling, and Brie licked her lips nervously as she stepped back.

Ms. Clark leaned in even closer. "Maybe it has something to do with the fact such talented lips are wasted on you."

Brie had no quick comeback and had to watch silently as Sir said goodbye while he escorted Ms. Clark to the door.

The moment it closed, Sir turned around and said with a devilish smirk, "On your knees, now."

Brie sank down to the floor, automatically putting

her hands behind her back.

Sir began unbuckling his belt as he approached. "Those talented lips are definitely *not* wasted on you."

The next goodbye was much more expected and enjoyable. Sir and Brie met with his mother in his lawyer's downtown office. Ruth had complained that it was far too stuffy and impersonal, which was exactly the reason Sir had chosen it.

When they entered the room, Sir asked Mr. Thompson straight away, "Are the papers ready?"

"Of course," he said, handing Sir the stack of documents.

"Excellent. Let's get started."

Ruth did not seem to care for his abruptness. "Wait one second, son. I think we need to have a little discussion first."

"This is the discussion. The terms are simple. I will provide you with transportation and supplies if you agree to go to China for three years as a medical volunteer."

"That is not having a discussion; that is telling me what to do. I'm your mother, damn it. I don't deserve to be treated like a common business transaction."

"I see no mother before me. What I see is a manipulative, self-centered beast with a total lack of a conscience. I hope the work you do over the next three years opens your eyes to the truth."

"Fuck you, Thane. And I'm not going to some third

world country!"

Sir shrugged his shoulders, pushing the papers towards her. "You don't have to. However, people are out for blood, Ruth. I'm giving you a fresh start because I need to believe there is a human heart beating somewhere in that chest." He pushed a pen towards her. "You can worry where your next meal or lawsuit is coming from, or you can sign this and be gone within the hour. Your choice."

"I won't do it. At least not until we speak. Alone."

He pushed back his sleeve to glance at his watch. "You have two minutes to make a decision. After that, the offer is rescinded."

"You are a hateful bastard." She glared at Brie. "This will be you one day, girl. One day you'll be sitting in a lawyer's office, being told that you are no longer loved."

Sir cleared his throat. "One minute and forty seconds."

Ruth looked startled and grabbed the papers, looking them over. "Will I get an allowance afterwards?"

"No, you are only being supported for the three years you volunteer. After that, you are on your own. No contact with either of us will be tolerated on your return," he said, glancing in Brie's direction.

"Why would I ever sign this?"

"Because you have burned all your bridges. Show the public you're genuinely sorry for manipulating their good hearts by taking this time to give to others. Possibly in three years they will have forgiven you, or forgotten that you exist. It's a win-win, either way."

She looked at the document again and whined like a

spoiled child, "But I don't want to go to China."

"Thirty seconds," Sir answered.

Ruth quickly scribbled her name on every page, then threw them at Sir. "Bastard!"

Sir gathered the papers and handed them to Mr. Thompson. He stood up without acknowledging her again, calmly walking Brie to the door.

Ruth came unglued. "Don't walk away from me, Thane. Don't you dare walk away from me, you fucking coward. You're a failure as a man. Everyone knows it. Beating up little girls and abandoning your mother like this. It's disgusting!" When she got no response, Ruth screamed, "You should have died with your father! You hear me?"

Sir opened the door without pausing, putting his hand on the small of Brie's back.

Ruth redirected her wrath. "That money's mine, bitch. Don't you think for one second you're getting any of my son's money. I'm his mother; it's *mine*!"

Sir guided Brie out of the door and turned to face the beast. "But I have no mother."

He shut the door on a torrent of profanities.

Sir winked at Brie. "Satisfying on so many levels."

Brie tightened her grip on him, extremely proud of the way he had handled the wretched woman. Sir had been compassionate without giving an inch of his soul.

He let out a long, ragged sigh as they waited for the elevator. "The beast is no longer my problem." Sir gave Brie a cheerless smile. "From now on, when I remember Ruth Davis, I will think of the woman my father once loved. The reality is that I lost both of my parents when I was a boy."

When they returned home, Sir quietly put the framed picture of his father in the living room. It marked his emancipation.

Pearls

S ir's involvement with the documentary had caused his business to take a severe financial hit—a hit that would take years to recover from. Brie was shocked when he listed the number of clients he'd lost during a discussion with Master Anderson.

"Impressive," Master Anderson commented, showing only amusement at the amount.

But Brie was devastated. "I feel horrible, Sir. I never thought my film would impact your business so negatively."

He looked at her with compassion. "I always knew there'd be a significant cost, Brie. It's an investment I was prepared to make. I realized it would obligate me to pursue clients outside the States to offset the losses." When he saw her continued distress, he gestured for her to kneel beside him. "Unlike you—a girl who tends to make impulsive decisions based on her heart—I weigh the risks and act accordingly."

She rested her head on his thigh. "I do admire how you calculate the costs, Sir. It's as if you play a game of chess with life."

Master Anderson laughed at the statement. "Yes, that's exactly what you do, Thane."

Sir sounded amused. "I'm not sure I care for the analogy, Brie. However, it *is* true that while you are constantly surprised by the aftermath of your decisions, I rarely am."

"You're very wise, Sir."

"Tsk, tsk," Sir said as warning before lifting Brie over his knee, raising her skirt. "What did I say about that word?"

Brie struggled not to smile when she apologized. "I'm sorry, Sir. Not wise, definitely not wise. I meant knowledgeable."

He smacked her hard on the ass. "Try again."

"Sage-like."

"No." He spanked her even harder.

"Intelligent! Intelligent!" she squeaked.

He rubbed his hand over her red ass. "Acceptable." He pulled her skirt back down and returned her to her kneeling position.

Sir spoke to Master Anderson as if nothing had happened. "When will you be leaving?"

"By the end of the month. I already have a warehouse in mind. I plan to be there before renovations start."

Sir chuckled. "I'm certain your neighbors are going to miss you."

"It has been impossible. I tell you, ever since the documentary, the women won't leave me alone. What started out as harmless flirtation has quickly turned into cougar wars. Best to leave before someone gets hurt."

"Or shot."

Master Anderson grinned smugly, but his smile fell when he saw the herb garden on the counter. "Thane, I gave you this garden to take care of." He walked over and caressed the yellowing leaves. "They're screaming for light. You can't expect them to produce a pleasant flavor if you don't give them the food they require." Without asking, he moved an end table near the window and placed the small herb garden on it. "There. Now the plants will be happy, but you'll have to water them more."

Sir growled with irritation. "I never asked for a garden."

"But you *will* care for it. Think of it as a part of me when I'm gone."

"Great. Then I'll be sure to flick the leaves and poke the roots every time I water," Sir said sarcastically.

"As long as you water me, I'm okay with being flicked and poked."

Brie giggled on Sir's thigh.

Master Anderson glanced at his watch. "Unfortunately, as much fun as I'm having entertaining young Brie here, I can't stay longer."

Sir stroked Brie's hair one last time before he got up to see his friend out. "I trust you're still coming tonight."

"Of course. Wouldn't miss it."

Brie was pleased to hear that Master Anderson would be there. She'd been looking forward to the huge party at the Training Center all week. It was going to be the biggest gathering to date. Sir had said the film had been great for the Center, but the increased enrollment necessitated an expansion. A whole new wing was being built at the college to accommodate future classes. Everyone associated with the Center would be there to celebrate.

In honor of the event, Sir had purchased a special gown for her. "It only makes sense that the woman responsible for the expansion looks stunning for the party."

The gown was a black, sequined seduction with a high, modest neckline in the front and a low back that exposed the barest peek of her brand. Sir seemed to find it highly erotic, and kept grazing his hand over her mark.

Before they left, he surprised her by removing the condor necklace. Brie protested, "But I love that, Sir."

"Tonight you only wear your collar and this around your neck," he replied, holding up her strand of pearls. He looped it once and let the length drape gracefully down her back.

"My goddess, my slut," Sir murmured as he lightly bit her shoulder.

Oh, this was going to be a grand celebration indeed!

When they pulled up to the Training Center, Sir parked his Lotus in his old spot—reserved exclusively for the headmaster. Sir chuckled as he got out, stating, "Coen needs a little aggravation."

They'd come early to help with the set-up, but the commons area was already decorated with layers of black and iridescent pearl, giving an air of sophistication to the festivities.

Brie touched the hanging silks and cooed. "Wow, I love how elegant this looks, Sir. Very classy."

"Class is a given for anything associated with the Center," he responded with a smirk.

It took a second before she got his joke and started laughing, but Headmaster Coen cut her merriment short when he entered.

"Very funny, Davis. Repark your car *now.*"

"You can't be serious."

The headmaster responded angrily, "I assure you, I'm quite serious."

Sir grinned like a mischievous schoolboy as he fished his car keys out of his pocket. He gave Brie free rein to explore the Center while he went to change parking spots.

As she walked down the silent halls, Brie was bombarded with memories: Baron's initial challenge and those damn six-inch heels. The experience of her first auction with Rytsar, followed by lessons on deep-throating. She'd learned to overcome her fear of the cane with Marquis, and discovered the joy of flying under Tono's skilled hands.

She made her way back to the commons, running her fingers against the wall and smiling to herself as she passed the bondage room. She remembered her second night at the Center, waiting in the hallway for Sir to unlock the door after class…

Good memories.

She was determined to drag Mary and Lea back here

while the party was going on. It would be fun to reminisce together. Now that the film was complete and all the excitement of the release was over, she needed to set aside girl-time on a regular basis.

Brie was startled to see the silhouette of a man standing in the hallway ahead of her. It was definitely not Sir. She stopped in her tracks until she heard a hearty, "*Radost moya!*"

"Rytsar!" she cried, running to his open arms. "I had no idea you would be here tonight."

The Russian picked her up, laughing. "I am part of the Training Center experience, am I not?"

"Well…you are for me," she answered, struggling to breathe inside his powerful embrace.

Such a sadist.

When he had nearly squeezed the breath out of her, he set her down, chuckling to himself. "Why don't you run off with me? I will teach you the power of pain and you can teach me the power of *lyubov'*."

"Hands in the air. Step away from the sub," Sir ordered from behind him.

Rytsar put his hands up. "We've been caught before we could make our grand escape." He turned around and walked to Sir, grinning like a Cheshire cat. "*Moy droog,* I am still convinced I could make her into a masochist. I just need a few weeks alone with her."

Sir held out his hand to Brie as he replied, "Not going to happen, my friend."

Walking down the hallway with a Dominant on either side brought back memories of the cabin, and a pleasant warmth grew between her legs. She looked up at the handsome Russian and thanked him for her extravagant birthday gift, adding, "Rytsar, the cabin is really too much."

He threw back his head and laughed. "Truth, *radost moya*? It has to be the most selfish gift I've given."

Sir snorted, slapping him hard on the back. "I suspected as much…"

Brie asked Sir, "Would it be okay if I tell him?"

"Why not?" he answered with amusement.

"Rytsar, you are the very first person to hear," Brie said excitedly. "We're leaving in two weeks for Italy and you'll never guess—" She saw the glimmer of hope in Rytsar's eyes and knew what he was thinking. "No, you're still not an uncle."

He frowned, shaking his head at Sir in mock disappointment.

"I don't have time for babies, Rytsar. I'm going to begin filming my new documentary."

Rytsar raised an eyebrow. "Another film?"

"Yes! This one will be about Alonzo Davis, the man behind the talent." Brie grinned at Sir. "Recently, there has been a surge of interest in his music."

Rytsar slapped his hand on Sir's shoulder. "I'm glad to hear it, *moy droog*."

Sir answered somberly, "Yes, it's time people know the truth about my father, and there is only one person I trust to tell it." He kissed the top of Brie's head.

As they walked into the commons, Brie was thrilled to see that it was already filling up with people. She spotted Mary and Faelan across the room and asked, "May I, Sir?"

"You may speak to whomever you wish tonight."

She bowed and thanked Sir before bounding off to talk to Mary.

Unfortunately, Mary burst her bubble about girl-time with the first words out of her mouth. "Guess our big news!"

Brie noticed the possessive way Faelan had his arm around Mary and felt certain she knew the answer. She said playfully, "Is there a certain piece of neck jewelry in your future?"

Mary looked mortified. "No, you idiot! You know I'm not ready for that shit. We're going to join a commune."

Brie laughed at her reaction. She could tell Mary wanted a collar, and the tight hold Faelan had on her let the world know his feelings. It wouldn't be long…

"So a hippie commune? That's cool, Mary, but I can't see you as a flower child."

Blonde Nemesis rolled her eyes. "It's a BDSM commune, bitch. Everyone works for the community, but the beauty is that you can live your D/s life out in the open. It's kind of like The Haven, but twenty-four seven. Just think, Faelan could come up to me while I'm peeling potatoes with the group, order me to bend over and fuck me, just like that. Nobody would bat an eyelid because it's totally accepted. The vanilla world left behind."

Brie was amazed. "I never knew there was such a place."

"Oh, yeah, it's up north. There are even a few couples who have been with that commune for years. God knows the things we can learn while we're there. Imagine living with a bunch of like-minded people—what could be better?"

Brie didn't like the idea of losing Mary. "What about your job?"

"I'm taking a six-month sabbatical, so it's no big deal." Mary groaned dramatically. "God, I'm so fucking tired of being hounded by idiots who saw the film. I can't tell you the number of vanillas hitting on me. Hell, both Faelan and I could use a break from that crap."

Faelan spoke up. "We're young and free to leave our jobs temporarily. Seems like the perfect time to explore the lifestyle in more depth, don't you think?"

Although Brie was not excited about them leaving, she hung onto the fact that it was a temporary loss. "Yes, Mr. Wallace, I can certainly understand the allure."

Mary's eyes sparkled with excitement. "Brie, you'll never guess what happens the first night."

Brie couldn't hide her smile when she answered, imagining Mary with a ring of pretty flowers in her hair, dancing around a maypole. "I have no clue."

"The day we arrive, they throw a huge party for us." Mary looked up at Faelan with a lustful grin. "At sunset, Faelan will bind me to the center table and present me to the community. Then they'll spend the whole evening sampling the newest submissive. Doesn't that sound wickedly hot?"

The idea of being taken by a group of Doms was both hot and frightening, but Brie was certain Mary could handle it. Ever since that night at The Haven with Faelan, she'd been different. She seemed complete, as if she had found a part of herself that had been lost. Mary could still be a bitch, of course, but she seemed like a much happier bitch.

Unfortunately, Lea hit Brie with even harder news. Brie could sense something was up when Lea hugged Brie so hard and for so long that her friend's boobs nearly smothered her.

"Isn't tonight exciting, girlfriend?"

Brie shrugged. "It's just a party for the new wing. Nothing to asphyxiate me over."

"Well, maybe not." Lea giggled. "But look around you. All this is because of you. *You* made this happen, Brie."

She waved away Lea's comment. "Nah, it was all of us. I just happened to have a camera."

Lea pinched her cheeks and wiggled them painfully. "Aren't you just so cute? Can't accept a compliment to save your life."

God, Brie had missed this—the silliness of being a girl. "Hey, Lea, I was thinking of starting up our girl-time again."

Lea frowned. "Oh, I'm sorry, sweetie. I'm going to be busy packing."

Brie's smile froze on her face. She couldn't believe what she'd just heard. "What do you mean?"

"I'm headed to Colorado, baby!"

Brie's stomach sank. *It's Ms. Clark all over again.*

"Don't do it, Lea. Please don't go chasing after Ms. Clark. Don't make the same mistake she did by running after someone who will never love you."

Lea laughed and gave Brie another hug. "I'm not, silly! Master Anderson asked me yesterday if I wanted to be a part of his new Training Center. I'm going to be the lead submissive for the trainee Doms. Isn't that awesome?"

Brie kept the smile plastered on her face, even though her heart was breaking. She couldn't bear the thought of losing Lea as well. "That's an incredible opportunity."

"I know! I'm so giddy about it I can't even think straight. And Colorado is gorgeous with all those huge mountains. Who knows? I just might become a sub-bunny on the ski slopes."

Brie could just imagine males crashing into trees as Lea skied down the slope in latex, exposing her ample cleavage to the mountain men. "You might be dangerous in the snow, girl."

"Hey, I hear Colorado isn't too far from California. I'm sure we can get together between my sessions."

"Yeah, that'll be great," Brie answered, but that sinking feeling grew stronger. She was afraid it wouldn't happen, so she said, "Let's set it up right now, before we get too busy and forget. I don't want *anything* to get in the way of our girl-time."

Lea bumped Brie's hip with hers. "You got it, girl-friend." She got out her phone and they looked over the calendar, picking the first date available. "Master Anderson has everything planned out to the day. I think the weekend after the school's first six-week session should work. You know I'll need to dish all about it with you!"

"Perfect, because I'll need to hear every detail."

Lea set a reminder on her phone. "All set. I've got you in there."

"I'm holding you to it, Lea. Come hell or high water, the two of us are getting together that weekend."

"Nothing comes between us, woman!" Lea assured her.

Brie hugged Lea again, doing her best to hold back tears.

No Mary and no Lea... Can it get any worse?

She sought out Mr. Reynolds and his wife, needing some stability to cling to.

When Sir's uncle saw Brie, his face lit up. "We couldn't be prouder. To think I had such talent sitting in my tobacco shop. I'm embarrassed I had you stocking cigarettes."

"No need to feel that way, Mr. Reynolds. I was happy to do it. Well...I was willing, at least."

He chuckled, remembering those days. "That damn Jeff. He was a thorn in both our sides."

Brie couldn't help herself and gave him a hug. She grabbed his wife's hand and gushed, "It's just great to see you both again." She was struck by a brilliant idea and prayed Sir wouldn't mind. "I was wondering..."

"What, dear?" Judy asked, squeezing her hand in encouragement.

"Would you join us for Thanksgiving dinner? I would love to cook the meal for you."

"I'd advise you to decline and save yourselves," Marquis commented behind her.

Brie turned to face him. "I've gotten much better at cooking, Marquis Gray. Truly, I have."

He patted her head as he told Mr. Reynolds, "Offer to bring the turkey, stuffing, potatoes, as well as the gravy and you should be good to go."

She crinkled her nose at Marquis and assured Mr. Reynolds, "I can cook all those things…"

If I google it, she added in her head.

Brie eagerly continued, "It will be lovely, I promise. Please say you'll come. Thanksgiving should be about family."

"And not about edible food," Marquis interjected.

She stamped her foot, biting back a witty retort. Marquis was a respected Dom and she knew her place, but he was being wicked with his teasing.

"Of course we'll come, dear," Judy replied.

Mr. Reynolds readily agreed. "It's an invitation we would never turn down."

"Great!" Brie felt some of her joy return.

Brie focused her attention back on Marquis Gray, noticing for the first time that Celestia was standing beside him. "It's so great to see you again!" Brie cried, sighing gratefully as she hugged the gentle woman. It was a friendship that held possibilities.

She was about to extend an invitation for Thanksgiving dinner, but Marquis Gray changed the subject. "I never did hear if you enjoyed the new flogger, Miss Bennett."

Brie shivered just thinking about it. "The flogger is incredible, Marquis. I've never known one to give two different sensations at the same time."

Marquis' eyes shone with pride as he explained, "I had that one especially made for you with a combination of suede and oiled leather. The flogger is also balanced so that the wielder can use it for longer sessions."

Sir came up behind Brie and put his hand on her shoulder. "It's the best flogger I've used, Gray. None finer."

Marquis seemed particularly pleased. "I have a similar one at home." He ran his fingers down Celestia's spine and Brie watched her quiver in response. "It's a favorite tool of ours." Marquis looked at Brie again and said, with a glint in his eye, "Wait until your present next year."

Tono came up and shook hands with the men before addressing Brie. "Amazing, the impact a simple film concept can have in the hands of a true artist."

She blushed at his compliment. "Thank you, Tono. It does amaze me that the Center is expanding and a new one is starting up because of the demand for training. I never guessed my documentary could effect that kind of change."

"That reminds me, Ren," Sir said, "I've heard rumors that you are going to start a national tour soon. Is that true?"

Tono glanced at Brie before he replied. "Yes. I've been contacted by a group of Kinbaku artists. Due to the increased interest, they are holding performances nationwide to promote understanding of the ancient art. I've been asked to lead it."

Brie's heart sank. *Not Tono too…*

She hid her disappointment, but felt compelled to ask, "Tono, you told me once that you preferred remaining in one place. What's changed?"

His smile was gentle when he answered, "I've become stagnant."

The meaning behind his answer was clear. He would be traveling the country to find the woman meant to be his complement.

"I wish you much success with the tour, Tono Nosaka," Brie said, bowing to him not as a submissive, but as a friend. She turned away, fighting to control her swirling emotions.

It was too much. Too many losses to swallow in one day.

Sir cupped his hand lightly over the brand on her back. "It's time, Brie." He led her to the stage.

As she mounted the steps, Brie forced herself to focus on the school's success so that her smile was genuine when she faced the large group. She scanned the crowd, and did a double-take when she saw two familiar faces she hadn't expected.

What are my parents doing here?

Sir put his arm around her waist and began, "I know many of you are familiar with the courage that burns inside the young woman who stands beside me." He looked down at Brie and stated proudly, "If you know her, then you know she has the heart of a lioness."

She burned with a heated blush, embarrassed to be praised so highly for her simple documentary.

Sir took his eyes off her to address the group again. "You may recall that a certain graduate of this school broke all protocol to offer her collar at my feet. You may also remember that it was *not* met with enthusiasm."

Several people chuckled in the crowd.

"I believe courage should be met with courage," Sir stated firmly. He reached into his pocket and pulled out a small box.

Brie watched in shock as he got down on one knee and held out the opened box. "Brianna Bennett, in front of everyone here, I am asking for your hand in marriage."

She glanced at the diamond ring nestled within. It sparkled with an eternity of promise.

When she looked back at Sir, time stopped. She took in the sight of her Master. It didn't seem right, seeing Sir on his knee before her in front of the people she knew and loved, but at the same time it was heartbreakingly beautiful.

For one fraction of a second—just one—she toyed with the idea of turning him down as payback.

But Brie's answer was loud and clear, so that there would be no doubt. "Yes, Thane Davis. I accept your proposal with all my heart." Enthusiastic applause filled the large room.

He stood up and took her hand. Brie lost herself in the moment, aware of only one thing—her Master's touch as he slipped the engagement ring on her finger.

Brie stared at him in stunned silence.

Sir smiled as he explained in a lowered voice, "I asked permission to marry you the day your father and I spoke in the study. Needless to say, it did not go the way I'd planned." He cradled her cheek and stroked her soft lips with his thumb. "But I am a determined man, Brie Bennett."

She pressed her cheek into his hand and returned his smile. "I cherish your determination, Sir."

"I know your father isn't going to like this, but I will

not be denied," Sir murmured as he fisted her hair and pulled her head back, giving Brie a possessive kiss that sealed his rights as her fiancé.

Brie stumbled slightly when he let go of her, overwhelmed by the kiss.

Sir announced to the group, "Please sit down and enjoy the meal my friend, Chef Sabello, has prepared for you. We are grateful you could join us tonight to celebrate our engagement."

So tonight was never about the expansion of the school or my film. Clever Sir...

The applause started up again as Sir led her off the stage to speak to her parents.

"Congratulations!" her mother cried, giving her a hug.

Her father's response was to turn to Sir and demand, "Was that really necessary? You were doing well up until...that *thing* at the end."

Sir wrapped his arm around Brie and said unapologetically, "Yes."

Brie ignored her father's criticism. "Thank you for giving us your blessing and for being here tonight. I—" Tears welled up, making it difficult to speak. "This means so much to me, Dad."

Her father held his arms out to her and Brie gratefully settled in his embrace. "I may not care for your choice of husband, Brie, but I am certain he loves you. In the end, that's what I care about most."

She stood on her tiptoes to kiss his cheek. "Dad, right now I am the happiest woman in the world."

Her father squeezed her tighter. "I guess that will

have to sustain me when I suffer from doubts later tonight."

Brie spent the evening flitting from table to table, catching up with people who had been part of her training, including Jennifer, the redhead who'd been Sir's date the day they first met, and Greg, the Dom from her first encounter. *Everyone* who had been a part of her training was there—even Mistress Clark.

Although the Domme stayed behind the scenes for most of the evening, she came to Brie before leaving. "It seems congratulations are in order, Miss Bennett. Sir Davis is an exceptional man." Her gaze burned into Brie when she added, "He deserves an exceptional sub."

Brie chose to ignore the last comment, knowing the woman's history with Sir. She replied respectfully, "Thank you, Ms. Clark. I wish you success in Colorado."

"Yes… Well, thank you," she answered uncomfortably. It seemed that having Brie know so much about her personal life made the Domme jumpy.

Who has the power now? Brie thought, pleased with the subtle shift of control.

Before she could explore this interesting new dynamic, her parents came to say goodbye. She watched Ms. Clark walk away and suddenly felt an ache of sadness. She would miss the harsh woman. It was a disconcerting realization.

Brie was surprised her dad seemed cheerful. When questioned about it, he explained, "You know, Brianna, we had a chance to talk to Mr. Gray during dinner. He is a remarkable person. A man of deep faith and philosophical insight. We had a fascinating conversation tonight."

If there was anyone who could convince her father that the D/s dynamic was healthy and viable, it was Marquis. Brie glanced at her ex-trainer from across the room and smiled in gratitude. He nodded slightly, accepting her thanks.

"Shall we?" Sir stated, letting Brie know it was time to go.

Brie looked over the commons one last time, taking in the moment so she could remember every detail. Then she looked down at her ring and smiled. "We shall, Sir."

Sir took Brie on a little detour on their way home. She was surprised when he parked his sports car on the side of the coastal highway and set the brake.

"Take off your shoes."

Brie did as she was told, wondering what he had planned when he took a blanket from behind the seat and slipped matches into his pocket. He went to her side of the car and opened the door.

"Come with me, Brie."

Her heart fluttered as she took his hand. He lifted her over his shoulder and spanked her playfully on the ass before starting down the trail.

Even in the dark, Brie recognized the beach. She'd been here before, and had mixed feelings about it. Brie fingered the pearls around her neck, remembering how badly the night had ended last time.

Sir made it down the trail quickly and, to Brie's relief, passed by the spot where they'd had their tryst. He took her closer to the water and set her down next to a fire ring that had been prepared beforehand.

He laid the blanket on the sand and commanded, "Lie down, Brie."

It startled her that he hadn't used her submissive name.

She lay down on the soft blanket and watched as Sir lit the fire. When it was pleasantly blazing, Brie held her hand out to him. "I'm so happy, Sir."

He took her hand and lay beside her on the blanket. "Tonight I prefer we call each other by our given names."

Brie leaned forward and breathed his name in his ear like a forbidden secret. "Thane."

He smiled, turning his head to kiss her. "I like the way it sounds coming from your beautiful lips."

Sir began slowly removing Brie's clothes, beginning with her stockings. He rolled them down one at a time, lifting her foot once it was free to examine it as if it were fine art. He kissed each toe tenderly before he started on the gown. Sir undressed her with such controlled passion that he made the experience another form of foreplay.

He took the pearls from her neck, rolling the beads over her body—first her right nipple and then her left, causing them to contract into tight buds for him. He trailed the beads down her torso, making Brie giggle with his feather-light touches.

Sir smiled as the pearls traveled southward and brushed against her femininity. Brie gasped, her clit already erect and hungry for his pleasure.

"Do you remember the night I was Khan?"

She nodded, smiling as she bit her lip in anticipation.

"Open your legs," he commanded.

She could barely breathe as she spread her legs open and exposed her sex to him. Sir stared at her, admiring her mound without touching it. She loved it when he examined her with his heated gaze. It made her feel beautiful.

Sir fingered her pussy, separating her outer lips, which were already moist with arousal. He placed the pearls on either side of her clit and pulled them taut. "You know what comes next..."

Brie moaned softly as he pulled the beads along, each pearl caressing her clit as it rolled by. She lifted her pelvis, wanting more when he had finished.

Sir spoiled her and repositioned the pearls to begin again. "Do you want to know what I see?"

"Yes."

"Your clit dances as I pull the strand down, and I am aware that each tiny movement brings a jolt of pleasure to you. It's erotic to watch."

She turned her head to the side and bit down on the blanket, lifting her pelvis again in silent petition. He granted her wish and pulled the pearls against her swollen clit one last time. Then he put them to his lips as he gazed down at her and ran them across his tongue, tasting her.

"I have another use for pearls. Present your wrists to me." Sir began binding her with the strand of pearls as if it were rope. It was not simply decoration. He bound her tightly so she could not break free.

"Put your hands above your head, Brie."

She stared at him, feeling vulnerable, naked and bound in the open like this. It was intoxicating.

Sir leaned over her and stated, "I told you that I would never marry."

"I remember," Brie replied, curious what had changed his mind.

"But I realized a simple truth after I collared you." Sir traced his finger over the collar on her neck and asked, "Do you know the difference in commitment between having a collared submissive and a wife?"

She shook her head.

He smiled down at her. "There is none. Even though I meant it when I told people years ago I would never marry, I hadn't met you yet."

A warm tear rolled down her cheek when she admitted, "Being your wife…it means everything to me."

He kissed her salty tear away. "It challenged me to grant your unspoken desire, but I am not a man to shy away from a worthy conquest. I had resisted the legal commitment because of my parents' past, but the simple truth is I was already fully committed to you." He leaned over her, his masculinity heightening all her senses. "The moment I locked that collar in place, our fates were sealed."

She looked up at Sir, admiring his handsome face framed by the stars in the sky. "I love you, Thane."

"I love you," he answered, as he began unbuttoning his shirt. He stared down at her lustfully as he undressed, revealing his toned chest first. She loved that it was covered in dark hair. He unfastened his pants next, pulling them down slowly to show off his muscular thighs. The last piece of clothing to go was his briefs. Brie smiled when she saw his erect manhood. The man looked magnificent naked.

Sir spread her legs and settled in between them. The head of his rigid cock pressed hard against her opening, demanding entrance.

Brie closed her eyes, savoring the feeling of her fiancé taking her slowly, a centimeter at a time. The peaceful sound of the ocean waves rolling in, along with the warmth of the crackling fire, added to the sensual moment.

"You are mine, Brie Bennett, spiritually and soon legally."

"Body, heart and soul," she murmured, sighing in pleasure as his cock slid in up to the hilt.

Sir cradled her face in his hands and demanded she open her eyes as he began rolling his hips. The depth of his penetration asserted his claim, but he was slow, gentle and loving in his taking of her.

He was her Master, but tonight he treated her as his goddess. Sir spent hours under the canvas of stars making love to her, exploring her body with his fingers, cock and tongue.

When she came, Sir whispered, "A lifetime to explore every facet of our love."

Brie gazed up at the stars shining in the night sky and smiled.

And this is just the beginning, Sir...

The Dream

Tono was laughing as he bound her in rope, joyous laughter that made Brie smile. He ran his hands over her skin, checking his knots before lifting her in the air. Her stomach did a little flip, the way it always did when he hoisted her upwards. She threw back her head, purring in sweet pleasure—there was nothing like flying with Tono.

"Breathe with me, toriko."

She turned towards his voice but, as she matched her breath with his, she saw a change in him. The joy in his eyes was replaced with profound pain and sorrow.

"Tono…"

The air around them became dark and empty. She found it difficult to breathe and struggled in her bonds. Without speaking, he lowered her to the floor and began untying her. Once she was free, he took the jute and cast it away. Tono glanced at her once, then turned, walking into the darkness without another word.

"Tono, come back!"

He ignored her, disappearing into the smothering

darkness, leaving Brie choking and gasping for air.

She woke up with a start and found herself still struggling to breathe.

"What's wrong, Brie?"

She couldn't shake the feeling of desperation. "Something's wrong with Tono Nosaka, Sir!"

At his urging, she called Tono's cell phone later that morning. She was surprised to hear a recording stating it was out of service, and her anxiety only increased.

"I'm sure everything is fine, Brie. I suggest you find out where his next stop is on the tour and mail a letter to the hotel where he's scheduled to stay."

Brie got the needed address and penned a quick note.

Dear Tono,

I've been wondering how you're doing. Is the tour a success and everything you envisioned it to be?

I sincerely hope things are well. I had an upsetting dream about you and just needed to check in.

Sending you thoughts of happiness and peace.

Sincerely,

~Brie

She folded the letter, slid it into an envelope and lovingly placed a stamp on it before handing it to Sir. "Would you like to read it before I lick the seal?"

"No, that is unnecessary. Although I will be interested in his reply."

She placed her letter on the pile of bills that were

going out that day and gave it one last caress before returning to her desk. She missed the Asian Dom more than she would ever have imagined. It was one thing to know he was on the other side of town and there was a chance of running into him on occasion at The Haven or the Training Center. Knowing he was on the other side of the world was hard, but even more difficult was not knowing how Tono was faring.

In her heart, despite Sir's assurances, Brie felt he was suffering and it deeply troubled her.

Breathe with me, toriko…

Sir was struggling with legal disputes involving some of his oldest clients. Sadly, he was still dealing with the negative fallout to his business caused by Brie's controversial documentary. It didn't seem fair that he should suffer for her career now that it had finally taken off. However, Brie was thrilled that her film had been nominated for several prestigious awards, and she'd already been on several talk shows to discuss it, as well as her personal experiences at the Training Center. There seemed to be a real interest building among the public about the D/s lifestyle.

While the spotlight was still on her, Brie tried to use her newfound fame to secure support for her upcoming documentary about Sir's father, Alonzo Davis. Although there was public interest in Sir as a Dominant, producers in the film industry did not feel it would extend to his deceased father, even though the man had been a renowned musical talent. Brie strongly disagreed and remained steadfast in her vision for the project, despite the lack of interest.

However, with Sir busy concluding the last of the litigation, Brie was left sitting alone at home, twiddling her thumbs. To pass the time, she researched Alonzo Davis through old newspaper clippings, TV interviews and musical recordings, but she longed to go back to Italy with Sir and get the information from the source—his family.

All that extra time also gave Brie the chance to worry about Tono. After weeks of silence, she tried to track him down online. In her search, she was shocked to discover all his Kinbaku engagements had been postponed indefinitely. His last known location was the hotel she'd sent the letter to, but after he'd completed his final performance there, Tono had disappeared. No one knew where he'd gone after that.

Brie was beside herself, but Sir assured her, "When Nosaka wants to be found, he will contact you. Until then, you must respect his need for privacy."

It was nearly impossible not to obsess over Tono's silence, but thankfully Mr. Holloway provided a welcome distraction when he asked for a meeting.

"Miss Bennett, it appears your film has struck a chord with the American public. We've received numerous letters and emails from fans of the documentary who are curious to know what's become of Mary since the collaring ceremony, and whether Tono and Faelan have secured permanent subs."

Brie chuckled.

"Viewers are also demanding more footage of Marquis and a session with Ms. Clark. It seems they're curious about her and want to see the Domme in action."

"She *is* a commanding presence," Brie agreed.

"Is that a yes, then? You'll do a sequel?"

Brie hesitated. Although her documentary had thrown her into the spotlight, it had also succeeded in labeling her as a director of kink. It seemed that Hollywood proper did not take her seriously, and the only interest in her had been for soft porn gigs, which was so *not* the direction she wanted to go. Would doing a sequel only help cement that perception?

"Let me get back to you on that, Mr. Holloway."

Brie remained unsure about working on a sequel until she received a heartfelt email from a fan:

Dear Brianna Bennett,

I can't tell you how much you've inspired me. I've been curious about the D/s lifestyle for years, but had no idea what it was really like or even how to find out. I felt as if I were with you as you discovered your strengths and limitations at the Submissive Training Center.

To be honest, watching your film made me long to experience the lifestyle myself. The men I've been attracted to all my life were bossy but they were not respectful like the men in your documentary. I realize now I want more than a dominant male; I want a man who prides himself on being a Dominant. I want to share that journey of discovery with someone worthy, and "gift" my loyalty and submission only to him.

I would never have had that life-changing revelation if it hadn't been for your film. Thank you, Miss Bennett, a hundred times over.

Bless you for your courage in sharing your personal journey, as well as facing those who would attack you and your Master for it. I hope someday D/s couples will be as socially acceptable as vanilla couples. Trust me, your film has helped to move public opinion in the right direction.

I will try to be as brave as you as I embark on my own journey.

Thanks again,
Lucy

Her email was not the first Brie had received—she'd gotten numerous messages and letters from people who'd enjoyed the film—but Lucy's openness struck a chord with Brie. Despite the public discussions on the subject, there was still so much misinformation and prejudice concerning the BDSM community. Lucy's hope for the future set a fire under Brie, kindling her interest in the new project.

The challenge now that she'd graduated from the

Submissive Training Center was to find a different focus for the storyline. The second film would certainly prove more difficult than the first since many of the major players had moved out of the LA area.

After careful consideration and much soul-searching, she submitted a proposal to Mr. Holloway with Sir's blessing. She anxiously awaited his approval; if Holloway liked the direction Brie wanted to take, she would have an exciting year ahead involving *lots* of travel.

She scoured the mail daily, hoping to see a contract from the producer. When that day finally arrived, she squealed with delight. "I have a good feeling about this, Sir!" she said, ripping open the manila envelope.

Brie started jumping in place as she read the contents.

"I take it he accepted your proposal," Sir replied with obvious amusement, getting up from his desk and walking over to her.

She grinned proudly as she presented the acceptance letter. "He did, Sir! In fact, he loves the idea."

"Well done, babygirl. You're well on your way." He kissed her on the forehead. The skin his lips had touched tingled in gratitude.

She looked up at Sir, basking in his praise. "Thank you."

He smiled, but his expression changed as he picked up another letter from the pile. "What's this?"

As important as the contract was to her, Sir was holding something of far more significance—her first contact from Tono since she'd written him. She knew it was from the Kinbaku Master because of the simple orchid sketched on the back of the envelope. It seemed that everything Tono touched was artistic and beautiful.

Instead of tearing it open, she carefully released the seal so she wouldn't ruin the painted flower. Brie pulled out the special rice paper and quickly unfolded it.

Dear Brie,

I was heartened to receive your letter. Your dream did not mislead you. I canceled my tour because my father is dying. I've kept quiet about it, as I do not want the public to know until he's passed. We are a private family and this is a private battle.

It has not been easy, as Otosama is in great pain.

Jute is my peace—my escape—but even that has been taken from me. Your letter, however, brought a smile. Thank you for it.

Give your Master my best.

Respectfully yours,
Ren Nosaka

Tears pricked Brie's eyes after reading his brief letter; the pain radiating from the printed words seemed to permeate the air around her.

"From Nosaka?"

She nodded, handing the letter to Sir. He looked it over, then slowly folded it before giving it back. "Your thoughts?"

"My heart breaks for him."

"Do you feel a visit is in order?"

114

Brie's heart leapt at the suggestion. "Really, Sir? Can we?"

"I'm almost finished here. Although I'd prefer to see it to the end, I'll talk with my lawyer to confirm he can handle the final details alone."

Sir beckoned her to sit with him as he moved to the couch. Brie glided over to her Master in only her collar, the skin of her naked young body tingling in anticipation of his masculine touch. She gladly curled up at his feet. With hands that soothed her soul, he began stroking her hair. "Nosaka has been there for us when we needed him. It's time we returned the favor."

She looked up at him, proud beyond words to be his submissive. "You are an honorable man, Sir. The best!"

He chuckled softly. "Maybe not quite as honorable as you presume. I plan to make a few calls and see if I can turn this into a business opportunity while we're there."

"You are as wise as you are honorable, Sir."

He raised his eyebrow before swiftly picking her up and placing her over his knee. He took hold of her wrists with one hand, holding them tight, and rubbed her naked ass.

"When will you learn, wayward sub?"

Brie yelped in pain when his hand made contact, but loved the warm feeling that dissipated from the area and radiated throughout her loins. She struggled in his arms as he took several more hard swats, the sounds of which echoed through the apartment.

He rubbed her ass tenderly, before slipping his fingers between her legs. "Wet with only a couple of smacks?" His fingers leisurely stroked her pussy, building her arousal. She stopped struggling, becoming still as she concentrated on the delicious feel of his sensual touch.

"I love my Master's hand," she purred.

"Do you, now?" He swatted her four more times, making her squeak in pleasurable pain.

"Very much, Sir."

His fingers returned to her pussy, slipping into her wet recesses. He knew the exact location of her G-spot and caressed it skillfully, causing her body to tense with an impending climax. "I wonder if I should reward your insolence with an orgasm."

She bit her lip, then replied playfully, "If it pleases you, Sir."

He chuckled softly. "It pleases me..."

Brie closed her eyes and let the orgasm roll over her. The rhythmic tightening of her inner muscles announced her climax, and he grunted with satisfaction. "I do love making you come, babygirl." He slapped her on the ass one more time, then commanded, "Present yourself to me." She immediately got down on all fours and opened herself to him, longing to be filled by her Master's shaft.

She trembled as he undressed and slowly knelt down behind her. He slid his manhood against her wet sex and caressed the folds of her pussy with the head of his cock, teasing her opening.

Brie pushed against his rigidity, wanting to be filled.

"No topping from the bottom, téa."

She whimpered in disappointment when he pulled away. It was hard not to be greedy for his shaft.

"Be still," he scolded lightly.

"Yes, Master."

Brie remained unmoving when his cock returned. Although she held her body in check, she expressed her pleasure in a purring moan. It still surprised her how much connecting with Sir in this way expanded her, making her joyously complete.

When he finally slipped his cock inside, Brie cried out in deep satisfaction. He slapped her ass. "You're a naughty girl, téa." He wrapped his hand in Brie's hair and pulled her head back. "So I will fuck you like a slut."

"Thank you, Master…" she moaned.

He grabbed her waist with his other hand, using it as leverage as he began to pound her hard, challenging her with his depth. Her body started humming with sexual electricity in response to his unrelenting assault. When Sir used her like this, she felt totally…completely…female. Her body became an instrument of gratification, his guttural growls of satisfaction her ultimate reward.

His fucking was selfish, rough and hard—everything she wanted at that moment. "More please," she begged.

Sir increased the tempo, making her cry out as her body began to ready itself for an orgasm.

"Do not come, téa," he commanded when her pussy began to quiver with needed release.

Brie knew Sir wanted her to concentrate solely on *his* climax. To add to his sensual pleasure, she began squeezing her inner muscles, caressing his shaft as he pounded into her.

"Fuck…" he groaned. Sir let go of her hair and grabbed her ass with both hands, having been taken to the edge. "Feel your Master's satisfaction."

Brie closed her eyes and focused on his shaft pulsing with each release of his come. She threw her head back and joined his vocalizations, the two of them united in their passion.

His Reality

S ir wasted no time arranging the trip to Japan after
the arrival of Tono's letter. He'd admitted his
concern to Brie. "His father's death will impact Ren in
ways he does not foresee yet."

Brie loved that Sir genuinely cared about Tono's
wellbeing. The two Doms had always respected each
other, but it seemed that because of their close connection with Brie, they were becoming real friends.

The plane ride to Japan was uneventful. Sir spent the
time calling potential clients to set up his agenda for the
week-long trip, while she silently worried about Tono. Sir
explained between phone calls, "These meetings will give
you an opportunity to spend time alone with Nosaka. I
do not think he'll be open with you if I'm present."

Brie wasn't entirely convinced Tono would be open
with her even if they were alone. He'd disclosed so little
in his letter, and it distressed her. She had to trust the
spiritual connection they shared was powerful enough
that her presence alone would prove comforting if he
chose to keep distant.

"Sleep if you can, Brie," Sir suggested. "You'll need to be fully rested in order to face the challenges ahead."

"I'd rather stay up with you, Sir."

He caressed her cheek before putting his hand over her eyes. He leaned over her, whispering, "Your dedication to your Master is charming, but I would prefer one of us sleep." She kept her eyes closed when he took his hand away, but she pouted to show her protest.

Sir leaned forward and kissed her, biting her pouty lip lightly before pulling away.

Damn, the man is sexy…

She almost opened her eyes, but remained true to her Master's wishes. Sighing with frustration, she curled up in a more comfortable position in the overly large airplane seat. Brie was lulled to sleep by the authoritative tones of Sir's business voice.

When they landed in Tokyo at midnight, Brie expected they'd head straight to the hotel, but Sir suggested they explore the city first and hailed a cab.

She found Tokyo fascinating. Driving on the left side of the road rather than the right brought its own unique, nervous thrill and she couldn't help whimpering every time they made a right-hand turn.

"I sure would hate to drive here," she told Sir.

He disagreed. "I'd find it invigorating. In fact, I should really get an international license, since I'm growing my international client base." Sir stared up at the tall high-rises surrounding them on both sides. "The culture here is definitely intriguing."

Brie was surprised to see a bright yellow version of what looked like the Eiffel Tower in the middle of the city. "What *is* that?"

"*That*, my dear, is Tokyo Tower."

"It sure looks like the Eiffel Tower, Sir."

"It's meant to. It's the most attractive antenna I've seen. I do like that about the Japanese culture. They take ordinary, practical things and make them appear beautiful, even artistic."

She snuggled against Sir, soaking in the excitement of the downtown area. The lights of Tokyo were far more colorful than in any city Brie had seen, even putting Vegas to shame. Every building was lit up with bright, vivid signs or animated screens. It appealed to her youthful nature, beckoning her to come and play.

"Can we take a walk, Sir?"

"Right now?"

"If it pleases you."

He had the cab driver pull over and told him to wait for them. Sir helped Brie out of the vehicle and placed his arm around her waist as he guided her through the streets.

Brie found herself subconsciously looking for Tono in the faces of all those they passed. Knowing they were in the same city made her feel as if Tono were close by, even though a chance meeting would be impossible in a place as crowded as this.

They walked up to an upscale bar and Sir ushered her inside. The walls were made of smoky glass with rich purple neon lighting up the bar area. Above, multicolored lanterns accented the ceiling, dotting the floor with their fun punch of color. She squeezed Sir's hand, charmed by the artistically modern yet playful decor.

Although the place was packed, Sir found two open seats at the bar. He ordered martinis for them both, then nodded his approval when he tasted the drink. "Damn fine martini. Drink up, téa."

As she was taking a sip, Sir discreetly slipped his hand up the inside of her thigh. She smiled as she opened her legs a little wider. There was an irresistible thrill knowing she was *his,* whenever and wherever he wanted.

Sir lightly brushed her sensitive clit, before removing his hand and dragging it slowly over his lips. It was his promise to her; later he would partake of her taste... She wiggled in her seat, her body tingling with sensual pleasure.

Brie glanced up at a large TV screen and was shocked to see an image of Tono's father. Although she could not understand what was being said, it was easy to follow the news story when they showed an outside shot of a hospital, then cut to an outdated shot of Tono and his mother.

Brie whispered hesitantly, "Is he dead?"

Sir shook his head. "No, but I believe the privacy Tono was trying to preserve has been compromised."

"Then we got here just in time," she breathed in relief.

The joy she'd felt just minutes ago was lost in a sea of new worry. Sir paid for the drinks and quickly escorted her back to the cab. "I hope you got the sleep you needed on the plane, babygirl. It doesn't appear you're going to get more anytime soon."

Sir spent several hours tracking Tono down. Despite

some language barrier issues, he not only found the location of the hospital where Tono's father was staying, but also a phone number for Tono's mother. "Unfortunately, we won't be able to reach Nosaka until the morning to inform him we've arrived," he explained.

"Tono knows we're coming, doesn't he?"

He surprised her by shaking his head.

"Then why are we here, Sir?"

"Nosaka is drowning. You sensed it, and his unusual actions confirmed it. The man needs our support."

Sir's pronouncement gave Brie chills, but the fact he had come to assist Tono touched her deeply. She struggled to speak, her throat choked up with emotion. "I can't believe you would do that, Sir."

"Nosaka is a good man," Sir said, wrapping his arm around her. "He should not suffer alone."

While he got ready for bed, Sir instructed Brie to undress completely, pulling her close when she joined him in the bed. "Everything will be okay, babygirl."

She pressed against him and closed her eyes, trusting him.

The next morning Sir tried to call Tono at his mother's, but only got a busy signal. "Not surprising," he stated. "They probably took it off the hook once the media got wind of the story."

Brie felt butterflies when they pulled up to Tono's family home, knowing that he had no idea they were coming. She hadn't understood the love and devotion the people had towards the famous *bakushi* until she was forced to wade through a crowd of journalists and grieving fans of the elder Kinbaku Master.

The home was charmingly traditional, with a large, decorative roof, thin dark wood accents and paper walls. Sir knocked on the door and announced loudly, "Ren Nosaka, it's the Davises."

Brie blushed with unexpected joy. Although they were engaged, they hadn't set a date for the wedding yet. Sir hadn't had time with all the litigation, and Brie hadn't wanted to push. However, she had to admit that hearing his last name associated with her was absolutely heart-melting.

It took several minutes, with the scrutiny of every eye on them, as they waited for the door to finally slide open. A petite older woman who shared Tono's facial features stood before them. Unfortunately, she wore an unwelcoming expression on her face.

"Visitors another day...please!"

Brie understood that was her polite way of saying "Go away", but Sir wasn't going anywhere and called into the house, "Ren, we aren't leaving until we speak to you."

When there was no movement or sound from within, the woman began to slide the door shut.

Brie called out, "Please, Tono Nosaka, I *have* to see you."

The door shut with a little added force, leaving Sir and Brie staring at each other. She glanced at the crowd of photographers behind them, listening to the rapid clicking of their cameras. "What do we do now?"

"We wait," Sir said patiently.

Brie put her hands behind her back and straightened her stance to match her Master's. The two stared at the door, ignoring the numerous shutter clicks fluttering behind them. After a few more excruciating minutes, the door slid back open and the old woman ushered them inside before quickly closing the door again.

It was easy to tell by her sour look that Mrs. Nosaka was not happy with their intrusion.

Sir bowed to her and asked, "Where is your son, Nosaka-*sama*?"

The woman frowned, but pointed to an open door down the hall on the right. Sir bowed again and smiled politely, choosing to ignore the woman's obvious displeasure as he placed his hand on Brie's back and guided her towards the room.

Sir cleared his throat at the threshold to get Tono's attention. The Asian Dom was bent over a small table, pouring three cups of hot tea.

Brie's heart fell when Tono looked up. His appearance was physically jarring—his face gaunt and hollow. He seemed a husk of the man he'd once been.

"Tono…" she whispered in distress.

He looked down at the teapot, choosing not to acknowledge her presence.

Sir quietly closed the door behind them and directed Brie to sit next to Tono. She sat beside her dear friend and tentatively reached out to touch his sleeve, but Tono deftly moved out of the way and addressed Sir.

"There was no reason for you to come, but please sit." He indicated that Sir should sit opposite him and placed a steaming cup in front of Sir. Without addressing Brie, he pushed the next cup towards her, then picked up the last one for himself, holding it up reverently to Sir.

"Although I appreciate the gesture of your visit, it was unnecessary." He nodded before taking a sip.

Sir looked at Brie and indicated that she should join them. She had to choke back the tears of rejection as she took a sip of the soothing green tea.

Even though Tono was purposely ignoring Brie, she felt the pain he was suffering and assured him, "We've come to support you, Tono Nosaka."

He shrugged off her words with a roll of his shoulders and told Sir, "I didn't need you to come."

For the first time, he glanced in her direction, his eyes devoid of their inner light. Brie was struck dumb by the depth of pain those rich chocolate eyes revealed.

Sir replied smoothly, "I'm sorry to see the media has become involved."

Tono took another sip of tea before responding. "We would prefer to suffer this battle alone with dignity, but even that has been taken from us."

Brie wanted to wrap her arms around him, but knew it would only upset him further, based on his behavior towards her. She sat there feeling useless while Sir explained to him, "I believe I can help if your father's doctors are willing to move him to another facility. Give me the go-ahead and I'll see what I can do."

"Although I doubt we can escape the paparazzi, you have my permission to try."

"How can I help?" Brie offered, determined to get past the emotional barrier between them.

Tono sighed, reluctantly meeting her gaze. "I do not need you here, Miss Bennett. Please go."

She couldn't hide her hurt and looked desperately at

Sir.

He gave her a private smile, commanding, "Téa, you will stay here while I make the arrangements." Before Tono could protest, Sir stood up and exited the room.

Brie sat beside Tono in uncomfortable silence. As he continued to sip his tea, she listened to his breathing out of habit, and instinctively slowed her breath to match his unique rhythm. Once they were in sync, she noticed his muscles relax.

Finally, he broke the painful silence. "Why? Why have you come, Brie?"

The tone of his voice sounded reproachful, but she answered his question in earnest. "Tono, the dream I wrote to you about has haunted me. As much as you may not want me here, I felt just as strongly that I *had* to come."

He closed his eyes and groaned. "You can't know how much your presence both comforts and wounds me."

His words cut her like a knife, but rather than reply, she took a sip of her tea and wondered, *What changed so drastically between us?* The two of them had developed a comfortable friendship despite their romantic past, but now it seemed all that had changed…

He pushed back from the small table and lay down on the mat, not looking at her as he spoke. "I was doing well, enjoying the tour, until I got the phone call. I thought my world was falling apart when I heard my father was in the hospital, but at the time I had no idea how serious it really was."

"What's wrong with your father, Tono?"

He snorted in disgust. "He went in for simple back surgery, but complications arose and he left the operating table paralyzed from the waist down. I arrived in Japan a day after he received the devastating news."

Tono turned his head towards Brie. "My father is a strong man—strong not only physically, but mentally. Even that prognosis did not deter him. He was determined to walk again so he could return to the art he loved, but fate has not been kind. A week later, he contracted a virulent strain of pneumonia. Now he fights for every breath and his body is growing weaker by the minute."

"I can't imagine how difficult it must be watching your father suffer."

He let out a painful sigh. "There's no hope. He will die from this, but he can't willingly leave this Earth. It is not in his nature; he will fight this until the end."

"As difficult as it is for you, Tono, his warrior spirit is truly inspiring."

"I have always admired my father, Brie." She watched in sympathy as a lone tear fell down his handsome face. "I'm not the warrior he is. I can't handle watching him suffer day in and day out. It's killing me inside."

Brie moved away from the table and sat next to Tono, taking his hands in hers. "I'm so sorry, Tono. Just so deeply sorry..."

"I wish I could switch places with him. I could handle that better than standing by having to watch him suffer like this. Every breath is a fight." He laid his head back and covered his eyes with his forearm. "I can't face it, yet I will again today, forced to make my way through the wall of media as added punishment."

"I'll go with you and push them out of the way if I have to."

Relief flooded through her when she saw him smile slightly.

"How is your mother holding up?" she asked quietly.

Tono shook his head, lowering his voice when he answered. "She has become unbearable. She feels as helpless as I do, but reacts by attempting to control things that are not hers to control. I spend my days at the hospital putting out the fires she creates. Naturally, her disdain is not limited to the nursing staff. All of us are an affront to her control. If she were not my mother, I... Let's just say I am struggling to manage her."

"Is there any way I can help?"

"You? No, your presence has only increased her distress."

Brie opened her mouth, ready to offer to leave, but he reached over and placed his finger on her lips. "But she deserves the challenge."

She nodded slowly, and his finger fell from her lips. Instead of dwelling on his mother, she brought the conversation back to his father. "I can't imagine losing my own father, but he isn't my mentor and trainer as well."

Tono closed his eyes. "Only those who have had an *osensei* can truly understand. My father poured all that he was into my instruction. When we trained, we were no longer bound by blood, but it was because of those blood ties that it meant so much more to me. I was his prize pupil and I flourished under his focused tutelage."

"If you felt that way, why did you end up leaving Japan?"

He smiled sadly as he sat up and gracefully crossed his legs. "Two reasons. I was interested in spreading my wings and discovering what America had to offer. I'd grown tired of others seeing me as only my father's protégé, a toy to be tested and critiqued for their entertainment."

"What was the other?"

"I could not stomach the relationship between my father and mother. Her lack of respect for him transferred to me as well. Whereas he felt the need to acquiesce to her, I did not. The only way to preserve the familial ties was to leave."

"It must have been difficult leaving your father behind."

"While it wasn't easy, I don't regret leaving. However, I do regret the time lost with him. Time I will never get back."

She put her hand on his shoulder. "But you're with him now."

He frowned. "Yes, we've had a few opportunities to talk, between the coughing spasms and the excruciating pain. However, our conversations have only reminded me how much…I've lost."

Brie felt he was holding something back, but she didn't press him to explain, grateful he was being as open as he was. "I'm afraid anything I say will only come off as a sad platitude," she apologized, squeezing him tight—*needing* to be of comfort to him. "I've never been in your shoes, but my heart genuinely hurts for you, Tono."

He lifted his hand and tenderly caressed her cheek. "I did not ask you to share in this pain, little one."

She pressed her hand against his, closing her eyes. "We're connected. Your pain is my pain. Time and distance do not affect that."

Unresolved Demons

The door slipped open and Tono's mother stood before them, eyes glaring. She spat out a stream of words obviously meant as an insult. Brie just smiled at her, getting up and walking over to the woman. Brie knew she must be hurting underneath all that anger, so she gave her a hug.

The woman's muscles churned underneath Brie's touch and she let out another wave of insults. Brie remained undeterred, laying her head on the woman's shoulder and squeezing her tighter as the woman struggled. She did her best to infuse Tono's mother with peace before letting go.

The look on Mrs. Nosaka's face was one of horror and offense. Tono stood up to speak, but was interrupted by his mother's vicious protests. The way Tono remained calm in the midst of her fury was truly heroic, but it was easy to see the toll it was taking on him.

Brie regretted her spontaneous gesture and hated that Tono was paying for it. When he had finished placating his mother, he sat at the table and slowly poured hot tea into his own cup, offering it to his mother. He then filled the two other cups, giving Sir's cup to Brie. He took hers and lifted it to his lips, indicating that they should all drink.

Watching Tono sip from her cup created an intimate and private connection between them.

His mother gave Brie one more disparaging look before accepting the tea Tono offered. Mother and son sat across from each other, sipping in silence.

They looked like two warring parties, not close family members.

Brie was relieved to hear a knock on the front door. When Tono's mother started to get up, Brie bowed and announced she was going to answer it. She could barely suppress her joy when she saw Sir standing on the doorstep.

"I'm so glad you're back, Sir," she whispered, as she escorted him down the hallway.

"You'll have to fill me in later," he stated before entering the room and bowing to both mother and son. "Ren, you'll be happy to know that your father is ready to be transported as soon as you give the hospital admin your approval. If you don't mind leaving through the back, I have a car waiting so you can join him at the more secure facility."

Tono nodded. "My deepest gratitude, Sir Davis." He then turned to his mother and explained the new arrangement. The woman became livid and started berating Tono. Although Brie could not understand her words, the venom behind them was clear.

It was not the reaction Brie had expected at all.

Sir seemed unfazed, and gave Tono a subtle nod before leaving the room with Brie. "I think I understand now what you meant about Ren's mother. He has his hands full with that one."

"I'm shocked. I thought she would be happy about the new arrangements you made, Sir."

"The fact is I chose not to discuss it with her. I must take partial responsibility for her negative response."

"Poor Tono…our being here has only increased his burden, not lessened it."

"I beg to differ, Brie. His mother will eventually see the benefit of the move and I noticed a marked difference in Tono's demeanor after the short time you two were together. Your instincts about him were spot on."

Sir smiled sadly. "No one should have to face such difficult circumstances alone, but it is hard to ask for assistance—especially for a Dominant. Our mission is to help Tono to temporarily escape this hell, even if it's just for a few days."

With Tono's god-like patience, he was eventually able to convince his mother to join them in the car waiting in a nearby alley behind the house. Mrs. Nosaka refused to acknowledge Brie and Sir, sitting in the front with the driver to avoid all contact with them.

It gave Sir the chance to discuss the details of the transfer with Tono. "If you agree, call this number and they will transfer him to the new facility under the name Haru Satou. As far as the press is concerned, your father remains at the current hospital in intensive care."

"Thank you again, Sir Davis. Both my mother and I are grateful, even if it does not appear that way at the moment. Neither of us do well with the media."

"Think nothing of it, Ren. I owed you one."

After a long drive through the streets of Tokyo, they arrived at a small hospital surrounded by a forest of bamboo. It had a secluded, serene look to it, despite it being surrounded by the bustling city.

"This is perfect," Tono stated as he got out and helped his mother from the car. As soon as they entered the building, Mrs. Nosaka began to interrogate the staff.

Brie thought her heart was in the right place—it was natural for a wife to want to make everything suitable for her husband—but Mrs. Nosaka's methods only alienated the staff who would be caring for him. Tono was already putting out fires, and they hadn't been there five minutes.

Sir made a quick phone call and told him, "Your father is ten minutes out. Why don't you wait outside for him and I'll attempt to manage the tidal wave of resentment your mother just created."

"It is not your battle to fight," Tono objected.

Sir put his hand on the Asian Dom's shoulder. "We are only here for a short while, so take us up on our offers to assist you." When Tono did not appear convinced, Sir added, "Do not dishonor me by refusing my request to help."

Tono cracked a rare smile. "Very well."

He escorted his mother out, to her vehement protests. Sir instructed Brie to follow, telling her, "Tono needs your calming presence. He's been stretched too far for too long. That serene look on his face hides a tempest ready to be released."

Brie had sensed Tono's tension as well, and hurried outside to join him. As soon as she exited the building, Tono's mother stopped her vocal tirade on her son. The woman glared bitterly at Brie, but she just shrugged and smiled, choosing to stand on the *other* side of Tono.

The three stood in awkward silence, while birds chirped and crickets sweetly serenaded them. Brie matched her breath with Tono's and noticed the tension of his jaw muscle slowly relax.

He winked when he caught her staring. There was nothing about Tono that Brie didn't love. He was loyal to his family and he honored his responsibilities with complete integrity, even when it was at great cost to himself. Truly, the man deserved an exceptional woman by his side—one who would support and love him completely.

She looked up at the clouds drifting by. *To the powers that be, could you bring Tono his soulmate? I can think of no one else who deserves your intervention more.*

Mrs. Nosaka snapped something at Brie, then turned to Tono, expecting him to translate for her. He cleared his throat, prefacing her statement with, "Take this with a grain of salt, Brie. My mother would like you to wipe that foolish look off your face."

Brie grinned, wondering what her expression had been when she'd said her little prayer for Tono. She turned to his mother and looked her directly in the eye, saying with a pleasant smile, "Tell her I will cease, and I'm sorry to have upset her."

Tono seemed relieved by her response and repeated Brie's words in Japanese. Mrs. Nosaka glared at her. She spat something to Tono, raising her eyebrow while looking down her nose at Brie.

"My mother also wishes that you would refrain from looking her in the eye."

Brie pursed her lips. So…she had another Ms. Clark on her hands.

I've been trained well for this.

Brie lowered her eyes and bowed before Mrs. Nosaka. Although she heard an angry huff, the woman said no more.

Tono lightly brushed against Brie's arm and she smiled to herself. She knew it was his way of thanking her for submitting to his mother. The simple fact was, Brie would do anything to help him.

A short time later, the ambulance pulled up. Brie stayed where she was as Tono and Mrs. Nosaka approached it. As soon as the driver opened the back of the ambulance, Mrs. Nosaka began her instructions and complaints. Brie tried not to laugh as she watched the ambulance workers maneuver around her as they tried to get Tono's father out.

It was shocking to see Master Nosaka. He looked so frail now, a ghost of the imposing man he used to be. Brie had to hold back the tears as they rolled him by her. She followed, and returned to Sir as they wheeled Tono's father to a private room.

Brie took Sir's hand and whispered, "I feel so bad for him."

"I feel sympathy for all three."

"Yes…"

Sir directed her to the waiting room while he made

her a cup of tea. The warmth of the liquid was appreciated, but what Brie really craved was caffeine. She stifled a yawn as she took another sip, finding herself struggling to adjust to the jetlag. Yet Sir looked refreshed and alert. It seemed almost inhuman.

"Do you ever get tired?"

He gave her a little smirk. "I'm used to international travel. It doesn't affect me like it did when I was a boy."

She looked up at him and grinned. "I bet you were the cutest little boy, Sir."

He rolled his eyes, chuckling as he patted her knee.

"I really wish I could have known you in your gawky teen years." She stared at her Master more critically. "You probably didn't even have them, did you?"

He shook his head knowingly. "Something tells me your tiredness is playing into this conversation."

"But did you, Sir?"

"Did I what?"

"Did you have awkward teenage years?"

"If I answer, will you stop asking questions?"

She nodded, purring with inner satisfaction.

"When I was fourteen, I experienced a growth spurt that left me overly tall for my skinny frame. I was referred to as the Rod for years…and it wasn't meant as a compliment."

Brie batted her eyelids, saying teasingly, "If the girls gave you the nickname, I'm positive they meant it as a compliment, Sir."

He shook his head, but couldn't hide his smile.

Tono's mother exited Master Nosaka's room and went directly to the staff desk, making a new list of demands. Brie was surprised by how well the staff handled it.

"What did you say to them?" she asked Sir as she watched the encounter.

He leaned close and whispered, "I explained Mrs. Nosaka's unique requirements and how best to handle them."

"Well, whatever you said, it seems you've worked a miracle, Sir."

"Let's hope—"

Sir was interrupted when Tono came out and surprised them both by telling Brie, "My father would like to speak with you." The last time the two had met, Tono's father had called her '*dame*', claiming she was not good for Tono.

When she hesitated to respond, Tono assured her, "He asked specifically for you."

Brie wasn't prepared to be rejected again and glanced at Sir. "Can you come with me?"

Tono explained with regret, "Visitors are strictly limited. *Otosama's* condition is extremely compromised."

"Of course…" Brie looked back at Sir with trepidation before entering the room. He nodded confidently, giving her the extra shot of courage she needed, but she fully expected Tono's father would ask her to leave Japan.

Tono quietly shut the door and led Brie to the dying man, who was covered in tubes, wires and plastic hoses.

"*Otosama,*" Tono said softly.

The old man's eyes fluttered open. He glanced in Brie's direction, although it did not seem as if he could actually see her, then he mumbled something she couldn't understand.

Tono told her, "He would like you to come closer, Brie."

She bent down and smiled at him.

"*Sumimasen*" he whispered, before he began coughing violently.

Brie was absolutely stunned that his father had just apologized to her.

She stood back and watched as Tono comforted him through the coughing episode, her heart racing as she realized how very close Master Nosaka was to death. Brie had never been around someone dying before and it frightened her, especially knowing what a strong person he'd been only a few weeks ago.

Tono seemed uneasy when he explained, "My father wanted to apologize for upsetting you the night of graduation."

Brie smiled at the old man again and respectfully said thank you, grateful for her exposure to Japanese anime when she was younger. "*Domo arigatou gozaimasu*, Nosaka-sama."

For the first time, she saw the old man's eyes soften. It was very slight, but brought her great joy.

Although Tono was smiling as well, his eyes did not reflect it. Brie assumed he was too consumed with grief and instinctively gave him a hug. Tono stiffened in her embrace, shaking his head.

Brie realized she must have broken some unspoken social protocol and quickly broke away, apologizing to Tono under her breath.

Master Nosaka called out his son's name and Tono quickly returned to his father's side. The old man whispered something that caused Tono's eyes to water. It broke Brie's heart to see him in pain and she glanced away, but when she heard his chuckle, she braved a peek.

"*Hai,*" Tono answered his father with a definite blush on his cheeks.

What had the old man asked him?

Master Nosaka lifted his hand slightly and Tono grasped it, bowing until his forehead touched his father's hand. Brie admired the respect Tono had for him; it was deeply moving to witness firsthand.

Tono bowed formally one more time before escorting Brie out of the room. She bowed as well, then waved goodbye as she walked out the door—a chill running through her as she realized this might be the last time she'd ever see his father alive.

Tono led her to Sir and announced, "My father would like me to show you a favorite pastime of ours."

"Besides Kinbaku?" Brie asked, surprised.

That mysterious blush showed up again, coloring Tono's cheeks when he answered. "Yes."

"Well, now you have me intrigued, Nosaka," Sir replied. "When and where?"

Tono looked towards his father's room. "It would be best if we did it as soon as possible. I hate to leave my father in this condition, but he insists. Are you free tonight? I can pick you up at the hotel around eight."

Brie was equally curious, and hoped her question would shed some light on the night's festivities. "Formal or causal dress?"

Tono smiled when he answered her. "Casual." Then he turned to Sir, adding, "A few favorite toys would be advisable as well."

What the heck does Tono have planned tonight? she wondered with delight.

Whatever it was had the experienced Dom's cheeks turning a light shade of pink, so Brie knew it had to be something exceedingly wicked.

They left the hospital soon after to give Tono time with his father. In the car, Brie began to cry.

"Did Mr. Nosaka say something unkind, Brie?" Sir asked gently.

"No, Sir. He apologized to me."

Sir raised his eyebrow. "Now that *is* unexpected. He's not a man to take back an opinion once it's voiced."

"I'm in shock as well, Sir."

"So why are you crying, babygirl?"

"Being in that room, seeing Tono with his father… It was both touching and heartbreaking. I wish I could do something to change what's about to happen."

"Death is a struggle, but it's a journey all of us must travel, Brie. As much as you may wish to carry his burden, grief is a solitary endeavor. The most we can hope to do is act as a distraction from the pain and be there for Ren later, when everyone else has moved on."

Brie thought of Sir as a young man, having suffered the traumatic death of his father with no one supporting him other than his uncle, Mr. Reynolds. The ruthless curiosity of the press must have been excruciating to bear at such a young age.

She suspected that as hard as it was for her to see

Tono's father dying, it must be churning up painful memories for Sir as well. However, when she tried to broach the subject, he immediately cut her off with a stern lecture.

"This is not about me, this is about Nosaka!"

She knew better than to press him, but now there was no doubt in her mind that Sir was struggling emotionally. When they arrived at the hotel, she squeezed his hand as he helped her out of the car. Brie needed him to know that she was there for him—in whatever capacity he wanted—and went on tiptoe to whisper, "I'm here, Sir, however you need me."

His eyes stared past her, as if he were being tormented by some agonizing memory he couldn't get past. It continued to eat at him, his face becoming stern and unyielding as they entered the hotel room.

In a distant voice he informed her, "I need to prepare for my meeting tomorrow and will most likely be on the phone for the next few hours. It would be better if you stayed out here and worked on your documentary while I retire to the bedroom."

Brie nodded, although the last thing she wanted to do was work on the film. She *needed* to be with Sir, to understand what was troubling him. She called out as she watched him walk away from her. "Please, Sir…"

He turned back, his voice almost cruel in its fierceness. "What is it, Brie?"

She lost her nerve and replied timidly, "I hope your meeting goes well tomorrow."

He narrowed his eyes, knowing that was not what she had wanted to say, but he did not question her on it.

Instead, he entered the room and closed the door behind him, effectively shutting her out.

Brie swallowed back the tears. Even after all this time together, there were still moments when he cut himself off from her. It hurt deeply, more than she wanted to admit. He'd insisted that grieving was a solitary journey, and it appeared he still believed that to be true—but she didn't—so Brie gathered her courage and knocked on the door.

"What is it?" he asked in a harsh tone.

"May I come in?"

"No. I thought I'd made myself clear."

She was shocked by his denial of entrance, but would not be deterred by it. She laid her head against the door and pleaded, "Please tell me what's wrong, Sir." When he didn't answer, she reminded him, "We're condors."

The door was yanked open, leaving Brie teetering as she tried to keep from falling. His eyes shone with unveiled resentment. "As my sub, you are expected to follow my orders, téa. Do you need a lesson in obedience?"

She looked at the floor and answered meekly, "No, Master."

"Good. We both have jobs to do. I suggest you get to work."

She dutifully returned to the other room after he closed the door with unnecessary force. Brie got out her computer and stared at the screen, unable to think about the film.

Something had changed; she'd felt it in the car. Her frustration only grew knowing she had done nothing wrong, but she reminded herself that she was a condor. It was her honor and duty to see her Master through whatever was tearing at his soul, even when she was required to take the brunt of his misdirected anger.

Brie was certain Sir would cancel their outing with Tono, and was surprised when he emerged from the room thirty minutes before eight dressed in a dark shirt and jeans.

"Get dressed and meet me in the lobby."

Although his voice sounded warm, his expression was still distant and haunted. As she walked past him, however, Sir put his hand on her shoulder.

She stopped, her head bowed but her heart gladdened by the simple contact.

"It's not you, Brie."

She nodded with tears in her eyes. "I needed to hear that, Sir. Thank you."

"Tonight we concentrate our efforts on Nosaka, since that is the main reason we came to Japan." When Sir took his hand away, the comforting connection it created disappeared. He left her in the hotel room with things feeling just as distant as before.

It worried her.

With shaking hands, Brie dressed herself and went to join her Master in the lobby.

Tono's Secret

Tono entered the hotel looking stylish in his simple black kimono. Brie noticed a group of young women stare at him and then whisper amongst themselves excitedly.

"I see you brought the requested items," Tono commented, glancing at the backpack Sir had slung over his shoulder.

"Just a few essentials."

"Perfect." Tono glanced at Brie for a moment, then back at Sir. "Is anything wrong?"

Leave it to Tono to pick up on the tension between them.

"No," Sir assured him, "but I believe Brie is suffering from jetlag."

Tono asked Brie, "Would you rather skip tonight?"

"Absolutely not," Sir answered for her. "My sub is in need of a little adventure this evening."

Brie smiled, nodding her agreement.

With a glint in his eye, Tono said, "Good."

His countenance completely changed once they left the hotel. He became guarded, speaking in hushed tones.

"What we do must remain a secret. You can tell no one where we've been tonight."

Brie's eyes widened, charmed by his mysterious behavior. Was there a Japanese BDSM underground? The way Tono was acting, she figured the club must be extremely taboo.

She remembered how stunned she'd been to learn that Rytsar was a sadist. Was she about to find out something equally shocking about Tono?

Brie shivered.

She took a long, hard look at Tono once they were in his car. She quickly came to the conclusion that he wasn't the type to indulge in extreme play. His spirit was far too gentle—other than his feisty bouts of spanking.

She was stumped by what secret Tono and his father could be hiding, but it pleased her heart that the elder Nosaka wanted her to know it.

If Sir was burning with the same curiosity, he sure didn't show it. He looked calm and collected, as if he knew exactly where they were headed, so Brie leaned over and asked, "Where are we going, Sir?"

"I haven't a clue," he answered, giving her a slight smile before staring out the window. She looked down at the backpack on his lap and decided that their destination was unimportant.

Sir was right in his assertion that the only thing that mattered tonight was helping Tono.

The Asian Dom's behavior remained aloof after he parked the car, leading them through a labyrinth of narrow alleyways deep within an older section of the city. The location seemed to hint at something illicit or even dangerous. Sir put his arm protectively around Brie as if he felt the same way.

The building Tono eventually led them to had a brightly lit sign and crowds of young people milling about. To Brie it looked like a dance club from the outside, but she was in for a surprise when they walked through the entrance and were greeted by a steep set of stairs leading to a dark basement below.

A young man met them at the bottom of the stairs and bowed to Tono before asking him a series of questions in Japanese. There was a quick exchange of funds, then Tono told them to follow as he walked down a dimly lit corridor with vividly painted red doors on either side.

He led them to the farthest room and opened it with a shy grin, motioning them to enter.

Brie had no idea what to expect as she walked in, but she was surprised to see connected couches lining three of the walls of the room, with a low-lying wooden table in the center, and a large white screen covering the farthest wall.

"Please take a seat," Tono told them.

Sir placed his pack on the table and sat on the couch, patting the area next to him. Brie sat by his side, although she would have preferred kneeling at his feet.

As she glanced around, Brie concluded it must be a private screening room for bondage videos. Tono picked up a remote lying on the table and the speakers popped into life as a list of titles in Japanese appeared on the screen. Her curiosity increased when he went to a shelf in the corner and took something from a box there.

He returned with an item that looked suspiciously like a smaller version of a Hitachi Magic Wand. Brie giggled as it dawned on her that he was holding a mic, which meant they must be in a private karaoke room.

"No way..." she giggled.

Sir looked at him with amusement, chuckling to himself.

Tono tilted his head charmingly and asked, "Do you sing?"

Brie shook her head violently. "No! I'm sorry, Tono. I can't sing, not even a note."

He answered her protest with an engaging smile. "Come on, Brie—come sing with me."

"I'm serious, Tono. I would only make your eardrums bleed if I did."

"Please..."

His earnest plea pulled at her heartstrings, but Brie couldn't hide her horror at the idea of singing in front of either Dom and stated firmly, "I can't."

Tono looked to Sir for assistance.

Sir shook his head as he lay back on the couch. "I must admit, Nosaka, you've surprised me with this one. I never suspected this would be where we ended up. However, if you are serious about wanting to proceed further, I suggest *sake* may be in order. We will need to loosen Brie up and heighten our own tolerance for pain."

She blushed. Sir had once heard her sing in the shower and requested afterwards that she refrain from doing so again.

"I'm sure she's not as bad as you claim," Tono insisted, but he heeded Sir's warning and put down his mic, picking up a phone on the wall instead. He ordered the *sake*, but after noticing Sir holding up two fingers, he amended the order.

Tono sat next to Brie while they waited. She couldn't help grinning when she asked, "So this is really what you and your father do in secret?"

Tono smirked. "*Hai*. Wasn't what were you expecting?"

"Well, when you suggested bringing our favorite toys, I naturally imagined something a little...um...kinkier."

Tono's smile spread across his face, lighting up his brown eyes. "I wanted to try something a little different tonight. Clients are only bothered if they choose to order drinks, so we will remain undisturbed for hours."

"Ah..." She glanced around the room again, noting the expansive couches as well as the sturdy wooden table in front of her. Sure, she agreed there was a world of possibilities for the creatively gifted, but still...*karaoke*?

"Did you and your father come here often?" Sir asked.

"As often as our schedules allowed when I lived in Japan. It was our...secret pleasure."

There was a knock on the door and a striking young Japanese woman entered the room. She gracefully placed two warmed *sake* containers and three cups on the table, and bowed to Tono before leaving.

Sir sat up and grabbed a flask. "Mind if I pour? Since I've had the dubious pleasure of hearing Brie sing before, I need to fortify myself."

Brie felt the need to confess to Tono before things

went any further. "My singing is even worse than my cooking."

"I won't believe it until I hear it," Tono replied, taking the cup Sir offered him.

She giggled nervously as Sir handed over her *sake*, trying to quell the butterflies when she lifted the cup in reverence, then swallowed the warm liquid.

Brie noted with amusement how Sir reminded her of Rytsar in the way he quickly refilled the cups each time they drank. By the time her Master stopped pouring, both Doms had become unusually open and chatty.

"What an odd activity to share with your father, Ren," Sir stated. "I never pictured you as a singer."

He shrugged. "To me it's no different than going fishing or hunting like you Americans do with your fathers. It's simply a bonding experience between generations—one that only he and I shared." He smiled sadly, looking around the room. "Here my father was not my *otosama* and I was not his protégé. We were equals, sharing a mutual passion."

"I find it oddly fascinating…" Sir mused. "Do you consider yourself a good singer, Nosaka?"

"I'm fair. Not quite at the level of my father, but I've heard no complaints."

Sir snorted. "Is that because you normally tie and gag your audience?"

Tono burst out laughing. "Well, there's only one way to find out if I speak the truth." He retrieved another mic from the shelf and tried to hand it to Brie. "Your time has come, little one. Let me hear this infamous voice of yours."

She cringed and refused to take it, hesitant to ruin Tono's good impression of her.

He seemed surprised by her reaction, but took it in stride. "Very well. If I go first, you will join me for the next song."

Brie glanced at Sir, hoping for an out. "Only if it pleases my Master."

Sir raised his eyebrow, but said nothing.

"I will take that as a yes."

Tono started flipping through the sea of titles, explaining, "You may find it surprising that my father is a huge Elvis Presley fan. I'm singing this first one in honor of him."

Brie grinned when she recognized the song *Jailhouse Rock*. The foolish grin remained on her face, until she heard Tono's voice…

It was smooth, deep and warmly romantic.

She couldn't help staring at him, her jaw slack in admiration. Her whole perception of Tono changed and expanded as she listened to the rich tenor of his voice. He delighted her even more when he added a few thrusting Elvis moves at the end of his performance.

Brie clapped her hands enthusiastically, begging for more.

"I would definitely say you can sing, Nosaka," Sir complimented him.

Tono turned to Brie, twirling the mic. "Now to see if you are as poor a singer as you believe."

She groaned in protest. "Tono, I will only murder that beautiful sound of yours if I try to sing with you. Trust me."

He handed her the microphone. "Don't think, just follow my lead and sing."

Tono switched the subtitles to English while she waited. Brie stood beside him, dreading the moment her humiliation would be made complete. However, she found herself laughing when an old song from the movie *Dirty Dancing* began to play. The ballad, *I've Had the Time of My Life*, had been a favorite of hers when she was growing up.

Tono started, his voice low and alluring as he sang the male part of the popular love song. Having him sing such a silly, romantic tune took away some of her anxiety; enough that Brie smiled at Sir when her part came up on the screen. She opened her mouth, and… Brie chickened out at the last second, only whispering the words.

Tono shook his head and leaned in close, singing the female part with her. With the *sake* in her veins, bolstering her courage, Brie stared into his chocolate-brown eyes. It reminded her of the time they'd danced together the night of graduation, when she had trusted him to lead her on the dance floor. What came from her lips was a tragic sound, but Tono cheered her on with a smile.

Soon Brie was relaxed enough to let all her inhibitions down, and she fell into natural rhythm with Tono, her voice following his. Although she noticed that he cringed every time she sang off pitch, he never lost his smile—not once.

Sir clapped afterwards, and poured them another round of drinks. "I'm almost there," he teased, handing them each the *sake*. "Just a little more alcohol will deaden the last of these nerves." He wrapped his arm around Brie, kissing the top of her head. "Wow, babygirl, you really *can't* sing."

She looked up and giggled, taking no offense at his critique because it was true. She shot back playfully, "Now it's your turn, Sir."

"I don't sing, Brie, you know that," he admonished. Sir turned to Tono. "However, I think we would both like to hear you sing again—solo."

Brie nodded eagerly.

"I won't perform alone," Tono said, riffling through the box on the shelf and producing a tambourine for Brie. She jumped at the chance to accompany him without her voice.

Brie faced Sir as she practiced tapping the instrument against her hip, trying to entice him with her lusty moves. Sir sat back to admire her, but he stared at her with distant eyes, as if his mind kept wandering else-where.

Tono explained to Brie, "Although my father is a die-hard Elvis fan, I prefer something more current and a little more country."

Country? Brie couldn't believe Tono was a closet country fan.

Although she personally disliked country music, the moment Tono began to sing *The Dance* by Garth Brooks, all doubts about his choice of music were silenced.

Tono drew Brie in with his voice and broke her heart with the lyrics of the song. She forgot about the tambou-rine in her hand as she struggled to keep her emotions in check when he sang the words, "Our lives are better left to chance; I could have missed the pain, but I'd have had to miss the dance."

"That…that was beautiful, Tono," she muttered afterwards, not trusting herself to say more.

He looked at her tenderly and nodded, before holding out the microphone to Sir. "Your turn, Sir Davis."

"I already said that I don't sing."

Tono answered him in no uncertain terms, "No one leaves the room without singing."

"Not going to happen, Ren," Sir growled.

Brie was disappointed that he was refusing. She'd never heard her Master's singing voice and knew this might be her only chance. Wracking her brain, she searched for a valid reason why he must. When it finally came to her, Brie smiled to herself.

"Sir, didn't you once tell me that you would never ask me to do something you weren't willing to do yourself?"

He shook his head slowly, rubbing the area over his heart. "I can't believe you're using your Master's words against him, téa."

She noted that he'd used her sub name and knelt down at his feet like a proper submissive. With head bowed, she held up the microphone beseechingly. "Please, Master."

He was slow to take it. "Understand, my willful sub, my song will come at a steep price."

She kept her eyes down, trying to hide her glee. "Since I've never heard you sing, Master, it will be worth any price I must pay."

Sir stood up, looking at the microphone as if it were a foreign instrument of BDSM he had yet to master. He announced to Tono, "This will be the only song I sing tonight."

The Asian Dom bowed slightly. "Understood, Sir Davis."

Sir stared at Brie for several moments before instructing Tono to find *Demons* by the band Imagine Dragons. While he waited for Tono to locate the song, Sir slowly rolled up his sleeves, one at a time.

Brie felt butterflies, knowing this opportunity wasn't likely to be repeated.

Once Tono had highlighted the song, he handed Sir the remote and sat next to Brie.

"Would you like me to play the tambourine, Master?" she asked playfully.

"No, téa. I want you to *listen.*"

Brie nodded, waiting with bated breath to hear Sir's voice. It was low and gravely, which perfectly matched the song he'd chosen. The lyrics to *Demons* were haunting and sad, unbearably sad…

Brie could not hold back the tears when she realized halfway through that his choice of song was meant as an apology to her. Sir refused to look in her direction as he sang of love and the darkness of inner demons that still haunted his soul. When it ended, the room was silent.

Sir put down the mic and turned to face her. She stood up and walked into his open arms.

"I don't mean to hurt you, Brie," he whispered, kissing her forehead. She let out a deep sigh of emotional release, grateful that their connection had been reestablished.

Tono watched their private scene play out before him, and said nothing as he collected the mics and tambourine, depositing them back in the box.

"Shall we go, then?"

Sir shook his head. "No, Ren. My sub has a debt that must be paid."

Paying her Debt

Brie trembled in Sir's arms, knowing that playtime was about to begin, but having no idea what he had planned. Sir let go of her and picked up the backpack. "Did you bring anything, Nosaka?"

Tono nodded, producing a length of jute from inside his kimono.

"That will do nicely." Sir surprised Brie when he abruptly pulled off his T-shirt, exposing his manly chest. Then her Master sat down on the couch, and with an ominous grin, he slowly unbuttoned his pants.

Brie ached just watching Sir undress in front of her. When he commanded, "On your knees, téa. Right where you stand," she instantly dropped to a kneeling position.

"Take off your top."

Brie gracefully removed her blouse and folded it, laying it on the floor beside her. When she looked up, he nodded at her bra. "All of it."

She unfastened her bra next and laid it on top of the blouse, waiting anxiously for his next order.

"Hands behind your back."

She thrust her breasts forward proudly, her nipples hardening under the appreciative gaze of her Master. The fact that Tono was also in the room only added to her excitement.

"Nosaka, bind téa's chest so that her breasts present nicely and secure her hands behind her back."

Brie's heart rate increased as she felt Tono approach and heard the swish of silk as he separated his kimono to kneel behind her. In a voice both commanding and calm, he ordered, "Wrists together."

Brie looked at her Master while Tono began the slow and sensual process of binding her. Sir's eyes remained trained on her as she was lulled and seduced by the jute.

Tono knew just how to caress and tease her as he placed the rope under her breasts, adjusting it carefully with gentle hands. The jute slid over her skin flirtatiously, tugging against her with each pull and tie of the rope, constricting her movement further with each new pass...

Brie moaned with pleasure when he laced the rope around her forearms and tightened it, forcing her chest farther forward.

"That's perfect," Sir complimented.

Tono grunted his agreement. Brie swayed under the Kinbaku Master's fluid movements, the call of his jute beckoning her to give in to its seductive power. She awakened from the provocative trance he'd created when Sir stood up, his cock stiff and ready before her.

"Come to your Master and open those pretty lips."

Brie moved slowly to remain graceful and alluring, as she made her way over to him on her knees with her arms bound. Once she reached him, she looked up at her

Master innocently and opened her lips wide.

He smiled down at her. "Do you remember the first time you sucked my cock, téa?"

She purred in response.

Sir eased his shaft into her mouth. "I want you to suck my cock exactly the way you did that first time."

Brie kept her eyes on him as she took his shaft deeply. Sir moved her hair to the side and held her head so he could watch her. She pulled back and took him deeper.

"That's it, téa…"

She swallowed, allowing the head of his cock to travel down her taut throat, forcing him deeper until her lips touched the very base of his shaft. Once there, she rocked gently back and forth, letting her throat caress his manhood with its tight constriction.

When Brie pulled back to catch her breath, she let him drop from her mouth and looked up, smiling at her Master.

"Again, babygirl."

Brie eagerly obliged, taking several deep breaths before opening her lips and taking him back in her mouth. This time Sir guided her using his hands, thrusting slowly. She stared up at him with love. Being taken like this took her to a different level of submission, one where she was purely female in the most primal form.

He pulled out and pushed her head back, running his fingers through her hair as he praised, "My good girl…"

Sir asked her to stand, then grasped her throat possessively. "I think it is time you attended to our host," he whispered, turning her around to face Tono. He undressed her completely, only leaving her collar.

"Kneel before him with your legs spread open."

Brie walked over to Tono, her heart beating faster with each step. The Asian Dom stared at her with an amorous gaze as she knelt down before him, spreading herself open as Sir had commanded.

"Please Nosaka with your lips, but do not open them, téa."

Tono loosened his sash and opened his kimono. Brie took in his toned body, then smiled to herself when she saw his arousal. She watched with admiration as he removed his underwear, exposing his erection.

Brie was grateful to be allowed the honor of ministering to his masculine need.

With lips that lightly teased, she kissed his cock, making her way from the base to the tip of his shaft. Brie looked up when she heard his intake of breath, and smiled when she saw the passionate look in his eye.

She used her soft lips to tease the frenulum and smooth head of his cock, then rubbed her cheek lovingly against his rigid shaft, like a feline. She bowed lower to give attention to his balls and to caress the perineum, the soft area underneath his scrotum, with feather-light kisses. She felt his whole body stiffen, his enjoyment of her attention obvious.

Brie saw a drop of his pre-come on the end of his shaft and rubbed her lips against it. She looked up at him, licking her lips seductively as she tasted his excitement. Tono groaned, his breath coming shallow and fast.

She turned her head and kept her lips closed as she rubbed them up and down the length of him, mimicking the motion and pace of slow thrusting. When he fisted her hair and pressed her lips harder against his cock, increasing the pace, her pussy tightened in pleasure, responding to his possessive grip.

That was when Sir knelt down behind her…

Brie moaned on Tono's shaft when Sir began to caress her clit, swirling her juices to slicken the sensitive flesh before briskly rubbing against it. Brie's breath quickly increased, meeting Tono's as they rode the tension building inside them both.

"Concentrate," Sir commanded.

Brie realized that she had stopped the motion on Tono's shaft, and resumed the pace she'd had before, looking up at him apologetically.

If Tono minded, his face didn't show it. He gazed down at her, the two in sync as their orgasms threatened to peak. Sir pulled his fingers away, allowing her to regain control of her body. Brie copied his actions by pulling away from Tono's cock.

Sir started up again, his touch slower and lighter. Brie shuddered, her libido now heightened and much easier to manipulate—just the way Sir liked it.

"Nosaka, reach into the bag there," he commanded.

Tono moved away from Brie, pulling out a large red candle.

"The lighter is in the front pocket," Sir informed him, as he returned to her clit and teased it relentlessly with his vigorous rubbing. "Place them on the table."

Brie held her breath, forcing her orgasm back as she watched Tono put down the beloved tools for wax play.

"Good girl," Sir growled in her ear, reaching forward and tugging on her nipples.

She groaned with pleasure and frustration, her pussy contracting in response to the manipulation, ruining her previous restraint. "Master…"

Sir chuckled, knowing that she was struggling to obey him. He added a bite on her neck to make things nearly impossible. Brie's whole body stiffened, so close to coming that tears formed in her eyes.

"Please."

Sir wrapped his hand around her throat, lifting her head so she looked him in the eyes. "Please what, téa?"

"Release…" she begged through gritted teeth, as he increased the pace and pressure on her clit.

"No."

She shuddered again. Sometimes her Master was a cruel man, but there was always purpose behind his actions—a method to his madness.

"Shall I test your resolve, téa?"

She shook her head, but answered dutifully, "If it pleases you, Master."

"I question your sincerity, little sub."

Brie took a deep breath, realizing he was not jesting. With renewed conviction, she responded, "It would be my honor to have my resolve tested, Master."

"Good." He swirled his finger against her clit, slowly and rhythmically, drawing her close to the edge again. Brie concentrated on a dark spot on the ceiling, putting all her energy into that black spot to get through his torturous teasing.

Sir released his hold on her and pulled out a Wartenberg wheel from the backpack. The smile on his face was dangerously wicked when he held it up for her to see.

The spiked instrument was a challenging tool, and her skin tingled with fearful anticipation.

"Lay her on the couch, Nosaka, with her head near the end."

Tono cradled her in his arms as he picked her up gently and laid her per Sir's instruction, adjusting her bound arms to a more comfortable position before he lit the candle on the table. She trembled where she lay, her pussy aching with desire at the thought of enduring both Doms' 'tests'.

Sir seated himself between her thighs and lightly ran his fingers up her leg. "Such soft, delicate skin…"

Tono picked up the candle, which now had a pool of melted wax. He knelt beside her and lifted the candle over her chest. "Close your eyes, Brie."

She did so, anticipating the burning drip of the hot wax and the wicked prickling of the Wartenberg wheel, wondering which of the two she would feel first.

However, the Doms were in control, and they surprised her.

Tono's gentle lips descended on hers as Sir kissed her inner thigh, slowly moving upwards. Brie was unprepared for such tender contact, and her control melted under their attention. When Sir fingered her pussy again, she lifted her pelvis out of his reach to prevent a cascading orgasm.

"No, téa. You must remain still."

Brie slowly settled her ass back onto the couch, gasping softly when his fingers returned. When Tono slipped his tongue into her mouth, her pussy began its prelude to an orgasmic dance without her permission.

The sharp prick of the wheel ran across the top of her mound as hot wax dripped onto her left nipple, shocking her senses and helping her to regain power over her body. Brie moaned, the explicit combination of pleasure and pain teasing her. The hot liquid rolled down the side of her breast before cooling into hard wax.

Sir rolled the wicked wheel down her left thigh, pressing hard enough to make her skin break out in tingling goosebumps while Tono brushed his hand slightly over her right breast, adding to her chills.

When the Asian Dom covered her nipple with the hot liquid, Brie arched her back in pleasure, loving the momentary burn followed by the ticklish trails the wax created. Sir focused his attention on her clit as Tono began crafting a simple design of a large flower on her stomach. The fact that Tono could excite Brie with the wax while making her a beautiful piece of artwork in the process totally enchanted her. But she tensed when Sir resumed his sensual rubbing of her clit as he teasingly tortured the sensitive soles of her feet with the wheel.

Sir challenged her further when he rolled the spiky instrument over the outside of her thigh and the shapely swell of her ass, applying more pressure than before. Brie realized she could fight against the impending orgasm he was building, or transcend it. She forced herself to relax against her Master's insistent caress, letting the fire between her legs burn hotter.

Rather than focusing on resisting the orgasm, she concentrated on the burn of the wax, the needle points of the wheel, and allowed those sensations to carry her.

"That's my good girl, fly for me..." Sir said gruffly,

kissing her inner thigh as he rolled the spiky instrument over the arch of her foot.

"Ahhh…" she gasped, welcoming the challenge of the Wartenberg wheel because it helped her to soar higher into subspace.

The smell of smoke from the candle signaled that Tono had finished his creation. His warm lips teased her, kissing her cheeks, forehead and the tip of her nose. "You are beautiful, *toriko*," he whispered, before kissing her passionately on the lips.

She opened her eyes and stared into his. The use of his chosen sub name for her surprised Brie and had an amorous effect, making her pussy respond with waves of undeniable desire.

"I think it's time to change this up, Nosaka."

Sir put the wheel down on the table and the two Doms switched places. Sir pulled her head farther off the edge and stroked her throat with his fingers. "I will fuck your face slowly, *téa*."

"Let me blindfold her first," Tono suggested, taking his silk sash and tying it securely over her eyes. It smelled of him.

Brie laid her head back down, now completely reliant on her other senses.

"You were successful in denying your desire," Sir complimented her. "Now it's time to embrace it—don't hold anything back."

She lay there, waiting. When nothing happened, she wondered if the two Doms were communicating silently.

OMG, what were they planning for her now? *Breathe, Brie, breathe…*

"Open," Sir commanded.

Brie parted her lips to take in his hard shaft. Her tongue met with the distinctive tang of Sir's pre-come—a taste she adored—then flickered against the underside of his cock. He pushed his shaft deeper into her throat and groaned, making her gush with wetness at hearing his need.

She was completely unprepared when she felt Tono's tongue press against her pussy. She moaned on Sir's manhood as her body violently released the pent-up orgasm she'd been so valiantly fighting. Her pussy lifted into the air of its own accord, bouncing up and down in rhythmic motion, in time with her pulsing orgasm.

Tono stayed with her, licking and sucking her clit as it quivered. She struggled against Sir's cock, her body unable to handle the intense stimulation.

"Be still," Sir commanded.

Brie froze, telling herself that to accept the intense stimulation, she had to transcend it. She forced her body to relax and embraced Tono's oral caress while Sir pressed his shaft deep into her throat.

A second orgasm rolled through Brie in a matter of seconds.

"Good girl," Sir praised her as he pulled out. "I want you to keep coming until I tell you to stop."

There was a time when she would have celebrated such a command, but experience had taught her how challenging it actually was. She understood that this was the very same test as earlier, just in reverse.

Sir eased his cock back into her mouth. "Suck."

Brie obediently began to suck, and found Tono

matching her rhythm between her legs. The synergy of the act initiated another orgasm, and Brie desperately struggled not to move as her body was rocked by it.

Tono murmured his approval. "Her come is so sweet."

"Again," Sir commanded softly. He grabbed her throat with one hand, pressing down on it as he began to make slow love to her mouth.

The feeling of total possession, forced submission and tender love-making was a combination that completely undid her.

Brie moaned as Tono brought her to another orgasm, one that refused to end. Her thighs trembled uncontrollably as she rode each wave. Sir added to the intensity by holding her in his tight grasp, his cock thrust far down her throat.

Tears of pure bliss were soaked up by her blindfold as she gave in to the continuous orgasm and flew…

"Come back to me."

Brie heard those words several times before realizing they were meant for her. She had to concentrate on following them. She opened her eyes and found Sir looking down at her, the blindfold removed.

"Enjoy yourself, téa?"

"Yes, Master…thank you."

"Thank Nosaka as well."

Brie lifted her head groggily and smiled at Tono. "Thank you, Tono Nosaka."

Sir caressed her cheek. "Now we will reward your tenacity, my sub. Swallow my pleasure while Nosaka covers you in his."

Brie opened her mouth to take in Sir's shaft, while Tono positioned himself, kneeling between her legs. She heard the slippery sound as the Asian Dom stroked his own manhood, while Sir began gently thrusting in her mouth, increasing the pace until he threw back his head and cried out.

Her muffled cries of pure ecstasy filled the room. Brie swallowed her Master's seed as Tono's hot come covered her bare mound. Having both men orgasm at the same time was a glorious experience.

Brie kissed the tip of Sir's cock tenderly when he pulled out of her mouth, then focused her attention on Tono's gentle hands as he cleaned his essence from her skin. Every touch was meaningful, articulating his thoughts without voice, and what he was expressing tonight was appreciation—and love.

Brie was slow to dress and needed to lean on Sir as they made their way out of the karaoke club and through the narrow alleyways back to the car. She was still flying from the encounter, and giggled periodically as they walked.

"What's so funny, Brie?" Tono asked.

She tried to formulate an answer but her thoughts were scattered because of the pleasant, lingering haze of subspace.

Sir answered for her. "She sometimes gets like this after an intense session. It's been happening more often lately. Unsure why that is."

Brie giggled. "Because I'm a very happy sub, Sir. Very happy."

Sir patted her hand, which she had wrapped around

his arm for support. The sweet gesture made Brie giggle again.

He raised his eyebrow, giving Tono an exasperated look. "See what I mean?"

Tono smiled. "It pleases me to see her so giddy. It is not an emotion I've encountered recently."

His statement reminded Brie of his tragic circumstances. The joy she felt fled her heart and tears started running down her face.

"What's wrong, Brie?" Sir questioned, stunned to suddenly find her crying.

She didn't want to ruin the evening, so she smiled up at him and stated, "I'm so happy, it makes me teary."

Sir gave her a private grin. "You are a mystery, Miss Bennett. One I believe it will take me a lifetime to solve."

A New Kind of Kinbaku

Brie was tickled that Sir had convinced Tono to perform part of his traveling Kinbaku act for them. Sir explained to her that getting Tono involved in his art again would help the jute Master to process the grief that was coming.

"There are times when you must be forced to do those things that are healthy for you. Nosaka will benefit greatly from the escape of Kinbaku in the months ahead."

Sir was always observing people and assessing their needs. Even though he was no longer part of the Training Center, that aspect of his nature could not be quelled. Brie admired that about him, but it also worried her. Sir was meant to train others; his natural talent, as well as his passion and experience, made him an exceedingly effective trainer. She hadn't felt guilt about his resignation from the Center in months, but now it returned with a vengeance.

Brie wondered if Sir still missed his position as headmaster. How could *her* personal training make up for all that he had given up? She shook off her doubts, reminding herself that Sir was an upfront man. If it was truly a problem, he would find a way to resolve it.

That second night, Brie and Sir visited Master Nosaka's studio. It was kind of eerie, knowing that Tono's father was fighting for his life just a few miles away, but it was obvious from Tono's countenance that for him the place brought peace.

Brie understood that this place was a tangible connection to his father, and wondered how many hours Tono had spent inside these walls, training and learning with the man. How young had he been when his training began? She'd never thought to ask him.

As she glanced around, Brie imagined Tono as a young boy, his long bangs hiding his lack of confidence as his father corrected him on a malformed knot. It made her smile to envision the scene.

Her thoughts were interrupted when a woman entered the large studio wearing a bright yellow kimono and dark red lipstick. She was young, like Brie, but with straight, waist-length hair and soft brown eyes. The girl bowed low to Tono, speaking words Brie did not understand.

He smiled, and told her to rise as he introduced her to his guests. "This is Chikako. She is one of my father's favorite partners to work with."

The girl turned to Brie and Sir and bowed again. In perfect English she said, "It is my pleasure to entertain you tonight."

Brie bowed to her as Sir answered, "We are honored to observe your scene."

Tono directed Chikako to sit on a jute mat in the middle of the room while he explained to them, "I'm going to show you a new routine I've been working on. Something that embraces the old traditions while adding a modern element to the mix. I hope to attract the younger generation to the ancient art."

"You have me intrigued yet again, Nosaka."

Brie felt a thrill of sensual excitement, knowing she was going to see Tono's mastery at work. "I can't wait!"

Tono directed them to sit on the floor as he pulled bundled strands of multicolored jute from his bag and placed them beside the girl. There was a psychological component to his placement. Brie knew the girl was already anticipating the caress of the rope as she watched him lay out the various colors of jute. Each new bundle meant another length of rope would sensually constrict her. It made Brie shiver just to think about it.

Tono turned down the lights and put on music to accompany the performance. Although it was his customary flute melody, this one had drum beats behind it, giving it an edgier sound. Brie smiled, liking the added element.

"What makes this performance unique," Tono informed them, "is the rope I am using. It has been specially treated to glow under black light." He switched on ultraviolet lights from above, and suddenly the rope on the ground glowed in a multitude of vibrant rainbow colors.

Brie clapped her hands. "Oh, I love it, Tono. I really love the bright colors!"

Tono smiled at her. "I thought it might appeal to

you."

"Very clever, Nosaka," Sir complimented. "Please enlighten us further."

Tono bowed slightly, then sat behind Chikako. He whispered to her as he gathered her in his arms and closed his eyes. Brie knew they were matching their breaths, finding their connection.

The young woman began to sway slightly in time with the music, the look on her face one of peaceful expectation. Brie was envious; there was no way around it. Any time she saw Tono performing his craft, there was a touch of jealousy—she always longed to be the one under his skilled hands, feeling the rope's seductive caress.

Tono whispered a command, and Chikako took a kneeling position. He took a length of glowing blue rope and tied her long hair into a ponytail, binding it in a pattern of decorative knots. Then he took the end of her long rope of hair and secured it to a ring above her. Once she was immobilized, Tono began to tease the girl by sliding the rope against her skin as he pleased her with gentle caresses.

In time with the music, he raised her arms above her head and bound them into an attractive ballerina pose.

As the music built in tempo and sensuality, the anticipation in the room heightened. From behind the girl, Tono took hold of the front of her silk kimono and waited, ripping it open at the dramatic crescendo of the song. The aggressive movement caught Brie by surprise, and she found it quite exhilarating.

She held her breath as Tono readied the girl for

flight, reliving that incredible feeling herself—the moment when the body leaves the ground for the first time. Brie moaned softly as she watched Chikako lifted into the air, bound in the glowing rope, the full beauty of the intricate bindings and her pose finally realized.

It was visually stunning!

Tono caressed his partner as he checked the knots, his movements in time with the melody. When the intensity and mood of the music changed, Tono's binding changed with it. He began to bind the sub roughly, slapping the jute hard on the floor, pulling and tugging on it as he tightly constricted her chest with his rope.

Brie trembled, imagining the feel of the forceful binding, and grabbed Sir's hand in response. He lightly trailed his finger over her skin, sexual energy flowing from him.

The feeling of eroticism between Tono and his partner definitely transferred to their audience, making it a shared experience for all. There was no doubt that Tono was on to something huge with this new kind of Kinbaku.

Brie's nipples ached as she watched the Asian Master possess the young woman with the jute. The act was raw in nature but, as always, Tono created beautiful art as he interwove the different colors, making simple designs that transformed into something unexpected and visually captivating.

He untied certain portions of rope as he went, turning the girl and binding her into new positions. Tono did it with such precision and speed that it became a slow dance as the young woman moved from graceful pose to graceful pose.

Brie was thoroughly entranced, admiring the strength of the sub as well as Tono's exceptional skill. It was easy to see how deeply she was under Tono's spell from the look of sensual bliss on her face. Brie could almost feel their connection—every touch, every slide of rope, every tug tingling on her own skin.

Tono gently touched his partner as he checked the knots again, his movements always in time with the song. Then he pushed her heel and the girl began to spin like a ballerina. Brie gasped, captivated by the pose.

"You like, téa?" Sir whispered.

"Yes, Master…"

His hand lightly brushed against her erect nipple, sending sensual shockwaves to her groin. "Feel my desire," he growled, biting her earlobe as he placed her hand on his hardening cock.

Brie moaned softly.

He placed her hand back in her lap and patted it, looking forward with a sexy smirk on his lips.

Such a wicked man.

Tono's light caresses and careful unbinding as he re-leased the sub from the jute were every bit as arousing as when he was tying her up. When he was finished, he held the girl in his arms and spoke to her softly as he kissed her.

Brie always loved seeing aftercare between part-ners—it was so intimate and tender.

"Shall we leave Nosaka and tend to our own needs?" Sir suggested.

Brie purred in approval. "Please, Master."

Sir went over to the couple sitting on the mat and quietly thanked them both for the scene, not wanting to disturb their aftercare any more than necessary. As Brie walked out of the studio behind Sir, she turned back and stared at the pair, wondering if Chikako might be the one…

Sir paid the cab that had been waiting for them, and took Brie for a walk instead. They made their leisurely way down the quiet streets of the neighborhood. It was charming to hear the families gathered at their dinner tables, talking and laughing from open windows in the numerous apartments surrounding the studio.

The full moon was so bright that everything was visible, covered in its pale blue light. Brie tentatively took Sir's hand. He squeezed it and smiled down at her. "Who are you, téa?"

She looked deep into his eyes and stated proudly, "I'm a condor, Master."

He nodded, gently affirming, "Yes, we both are."

Sir took a detour when he saw a park set in the center of the apartment buildings. They walked down the wandering path, taking in the unique beauty of the foliage tinted by moonlight. The night had an almost fairyland quality to it.

Sir directed her to sit under a large cherry tree, the sweet scent of its blossoms drifting down from the branches. He told her to lie down in the grass, then his hands began their exploration of her, passing over her clothing first before seeking more intimate access underneath the thin material.

She smiled up at him, adoring how cute he looked framed by the blossoms of the tree above.

"You are more than a condor, téa," he said, leaning over her. Sir added in a whisper, "You're also my babygirl." Her heart melted when he bent down and kissed her in the silvery moonlight. Their hands sought each other out, rubbing, caressing and teasing each other. The sexual excitement left over from Tono's performance only added fuel to their raging fire.

When Sir covered her mouth and growled, "Come for me," Brie shuddered in orgasmic release, moaning into his hand.

Afterwards she begged, "Now let me please you, Master."

Sir lay down beside her and unzipped his pants, putting her hand onto his stiff cock. Brie rubbed it, then stuck her fingers underneath the material of his briefs. She stroked his shaft with a slow, tight grip, moving from base to tip, just the way he liked it. When his breath became ragged, she added a twist of her wrist to bring him over the edge.

Sir grabbed the back of her head, forcing her lips onto his cock. Brie gratefully swallowed his essence, but as she did so she heard voices in the distance.

Her lips released their hold on his shaft so Sir could zip his pants. Then they sat up and he gathered her into his arms, whispering sweet nothings in her ear as the old couple smiled at them while they slowly shuffled past.

Brie waved at them, sighing in contentment. It seemed like a dream, being here in Sir's arms—the man who was both lover and Master.

Could anything be more romantic?

The Kiss

Brie spent the morning giggling over Japanese television in their hotel room, while Sir met with potential clients. Her sides ached from laughing so hard at the practical jokes played on unsuspecting bystanders—it was pure silliness.

Suddenly, the screen changed as the local newscast broke in. Brie instantly recognized the private hospital and a cold chill ran down her spine when Master Nosaka's photo popped onto the screen with the dates of his birth—and death.

She picked up her cell and called Sir to inform him of the tragic news.

"Go to the hospital," Sir instructed. "Nosaka will need you now."

Brie jumped into a cab, handing the man extra money and begging him to hurry. The cabbie had to park far from the hospital as a barricade had already been set up. Brie pushed through the reporters, as well as Master Nosaka's many supporters, but she was stopped at the door by security.

She would not be denied and started screaming, "Tono! Tono Nosaka!" when she saw him through the glass doors. He turned at the sound of her voice, then nodded to a staff member beside him. The security guard did not open the door until he got verbal approval.

Tono looked at her with a sad smile when she walked up to him. "Brie…"

She buried her head in his chest as she wrapped her arms around him. He was stiff and unyielding, his whole body shaking with unreleased grief. She looked up into his sad, chocolate-brown eyes and whispered, "Breathe with me, Tono."

He let out a subtle but heartbreaking groan. Her cheeks became wet as she cried the tears he was unable to shed. Brie squeezed him tighter, making a point to breathe slowly and deeply. She sensed his initial resistance, but in time his breath slowed to match hers.

They stood in the middle of the bustling hospital, in tune with each other, but oblivious to everything else as his sorrow became hers and her strength became his.

Finally, Tono whispered, "He's gone."

Brie nodded, knowing how great his loss was. Not only had he just lost a parent, but his teacher and mentor. "I'm so sorry."

Tono shook his head, fighting to maintain composure. "I will not cry, not here."

She took his hand and squeezed it. "Let's go somewhere private."

He led her out of the hospital, trying to guide her through the crowd of reporters to get to his car. To Brie's surprise and gratitude, Master Nosaka's fans pushed back the journalists to make a safe path for his son.

Tono drove away in excruciating silence, his grief overwhelming her with its darkness and depth. Brie struggled to breathe slowly as she accepted the onslaught of his crushing emotions.

He took her to Shinjuku Gyoen, a beautiful city park filled with over a thousand blooming cherry trees and the soothing sound of moving water. He walked with long strides, oblivious to her desperate attempts to keep up with him. She followed as close as she could while he led her deep into the park. Tono stopped for a brief moment when he came to a bridge before crossing over it to a small island dominated by an ancient tree.

There he sat under its immense branches and began to sob as he stared at the water—a black hole of grief Brie could not hope to penetrate. She settled beside him and the two sat in collective sorrow.

Eventually, when the tears stopped, he spoke. "Thank you."

She looked at him questioningly. "For what?"

"For being here, for not asking questions or trying to comfort me with meaningless words."

"I can't begin to know your pain, but this garden," she said, looking around, "it is a good place to mourn, Tono."

He tilted his head back and rested it against the tree. "It doesn't seem real. A man of great strength and wisdom is gone, yet the day continues unaffected." He turned to look at her. "It is both tragic and reassuring to me."

Brie smiled sadly.

"To never hear his praise again, or his correction—I can't fathom it."

"Neither can I."

He looked at her with fresh tears in his eyes. "*Otosama* is dead."

The pain behind his statement crushed her. "But you're not alone, Tono. I'm here with you."

His eyes reflected even deeper sorrow. "I wish that were true."

She squeezed his arm reassuringly. "It is! I'll always be here for you—both Sir and I will."

Tono looked deep into her eyes. It was the kind of gaze that was disconcerting because of its raw intensity.

"Brie, I…"

"What?" she urged when he stopped.

"I've kept something from you. Something I've been hesitant to share, even though it has been eating me alive."

"I *knew* you were hiding something. Please, Tono, I need to know."

He looked at her uncertainly, then nodded. "My father said something just before you arrived in Japan. Something that has tormented me ever since he mentioned it." He let out a long, drawn-out sigh, looking up towards the sky.

When Tono said nothing more, she encouraged him, "Whatever it is, I'm sure he never meant to hurt you. It's obvious that your father loved you very much."

He shook his head. "Brie, I've heard many words of criticism over the years, and have no problem receiving them from him."

"What is it, then?" she asked, suddenly concerned when she saw the look of agony in his eyes. What terrible secret had his father shared?

Tono groaned, hitting the back of his head against the tree and closing his eyes. "My father said he was sorry."

She was relieved to hear it, but couldn't fathom the reason for Tono's odd reaction. "Why would that make you upset? I don't understand."

He refused to look at her when he explained, "*Otosama* apologized for being wrong about you."

Brie's heart skipped a beat. She said nothing as the gravity of those words slowly sank in.

With eyes still closed, he told her, "As my father lay dying, he said it troubled him deeply knowing that he'd influenced your decision at the Collaring Ceremony."

The joy she felt that Tono's father had come to believe she was worthy of his son was tempered by the fact that it had changed the course of the evening—of both their lives.

Tono opened his eyes and turned his head towards her. "Thoughts spurred on by his confession have plagued me ever since, especially when my father admitted that you and I shared something he'd never known. He wished he hadn't taken that from me and begged for my forgiveness."

Brie stared ahead, reliving that night and his father's cold rejection of her. She asked quietly, "Did you give it to him, Tono? Your forgiveness?"

"Of course. It wasn't done maliciously."

Master Nosaka's rejection on graduation night had forced Brie to make a decision she hadn't been prepared to make. It had led her into the arms of Sir.

Tono stroked her cheek lightly. "If my father had said nothing, everything would be different, and that's what constantly haunts my thoughts now."

She closed her eyes, rocked by the revelation.

"Toriko…"

Brie opened her eyes when Tono's warm lips pressed against hers. She could feel his desperate need for connection—a connection that could release him from the pain and grief.

She instinctively pulled away and jumped to her feet. "No!" She ran from him, frightened by his emotional need as well as her desire to meet it.

"I'm sorry, Brie…" Tono called after her. "It was a mistake. There's no need to run from me."

She stumbled blindly out of the park, grabbing the first taxi she could find. Brie wrung her hands in the cab, wondering how she would explain it to Sir. Would he be understanding or angry, punishing Tono for this transgression?

In her heart, Brie understood the reason behind Tono's kiss. He was in agony and longed for the natural connection they shared to alleviate his suffering. The Asian Dom was a man of high principles, but in his raw grief he had given in to his human need.

She arrived at the hotel and anxiously waited for Sir's return. Rather than disturb him at his meeting, Brie undressed and knelt at the door. She contemplated how to break the news, praying she would be successful in swaying his reaction towards Tono.

Thankfully, all her worries were unfounded. When Sir opened the door and saw her, a slow smile spread across his face. "My beautiful pet."

He walked over and placed his hand on her head, stating quietly, "Stand and serve your Master."

She stood up gracefully, her eyes not leaving his. "Sir…"

He put his finger to her lips. "I know, Brie. Nosaka informed me what happened."

"It was an acci—"

He shook his head. "Although it was *not* an accident, I do believe it was a gut reaction to the death of his father." He brushed her cheek lightly. "I knew you would bring him comfort at this difficult time, but this was uncharacteristic of him. I noticed a similar breach of protocol when we scened together a few nights ago and he called you toriko. At the time, I had assumed it was a simple slip, him using his sub name for you, but now…" He rubbed his chin thoughtfully. "There is something else going on. I'm certain of it." Sir tilted her head up. "Did he tell you what that is?"

Brie met his gaze, although she was tempted to look away. She licked her lips nervously when she asked, "Did he share what his father said?"

"No."

"Master Nosaka told Tono that he regretted his influence during the Collaring Ceremony. He asked Tono to forgive him because he was wrong."

Sir took a deep intake of breath. "What a difficult confession for Nosaka to hear. No wonder he is reeling from it."

"You should also know that Tono apologized right after the kiss. He knew it was inappropriate, but I was so shocked by it that I just ran. My only thought was to come back to you and explain what had happened. I didn't want you to be angry with me—or with him."

"Brie," Sir said reassuringly, "there was no reason to worry. Nosaka is *not* Mr. Wallace." He played with a stray curl, smiling down at her. "Although we've been down this road before, you are not the same woman I first collared. You have learned much since then, and the truth is...I've grown as well."

She smiled as she laid her head against his chest. "I never want you to doubt my love, Sir. Never."

He answered her heartfelt declaration with a question. "I want an honest answer, Brie. Take time to think about it if you need to before you speak."

She hugged him tighter. "Yes, Sir."

"How does this new admission make you feel towards Nosaka?"

She looked up at him shyly. "At first I was thrilled to know Tono's father had changed his opinion of me. His rejection hurt me deeply." She let out a long sigh. "But then I realized that if he *had* approved of me that night, I wouldn't be here with you now."

"And that makes you feel how?" Sir pressed.

Brie told him the simple truth. "The moment you put this collar around my neck," she lightly touched the silver collar, "my fate was sealed. I want no other, even though I still love Tono Nosaka."

Sir leaned down and brushed his lips against hers.

"Good."

She smiled, crushing herself against his hard frame. He briefly returned her hug, but pulled away, stating, "Ren has lost his father today, and has compounded his suffering by embarrassing himself with us. I can't imagine his state of mind right now. Even though it will not be easy for him, I think it's best that we meet. In my eyes, what he's done is understandable, even though it broke protocol. I have no problem overlooking the incident, because he is not someone who will allow that to happen again."

Brie let out a sigh of relief. "I love being collared to such an exceptional man."

Sir chuckled lightly. "You make me nervous with the height of the pedestal you have me on, Brie."

She shook her head. "No, Sir, I have you set squarely on the ground. I realize you're human, but you are an incredible specimen of humanity—in many ways." She ran her hands over his chest and breathed in his masculine scent. "And I adore your modesty."

He lifted her chin, *tsk*ing. "Do not mock your Master, sub."

She grinned. "Never, Master."

He kissed her nose, stating, "Let's put Nosaka out of his misery."

The meeting with Tono at his mother's home was uncomfortable to begin with. It was obvious from his swollen eyes that Tono had been grieving, but one would never know it based on the serene expression on his face.

Sir held out his hand. "Ren, I want to express again our deepest sympathies for your loss."

Tono nodded stiffly as he shook it. "It was expected."

Sir put his other hand over Tono's and shook with more conviction. "Expected or not, it's still just as significant."

Tono grunted. "True. Knowing his death was imminent has not lessened the loss." He added sadly, "I'd hoped it would."

Brie noticed he was purposely avoiding looking in her direction.

Sir noticed it too. "Rather than dance around the elephant in the room, let me just say that I understand why you broke protocol. There is no reason for any tension between us."

"It was inexcusable," Tono replied, glancing briefly at Brie.

"No, Ren. It was unfortunate, but not inexcusable."

Tono turned to Brie, bowing before her formally. "I'm truly sorry, Miss Bennett."

"Such formality is unnecessary between friends," Sir said, patting Tono's back.

"Fine." Tono looked at her self-consciously and added, "I *am* sorry, Brie."

She smiled. "I accept your apology with a full heart, Tono Nosaka."

His mother interrupted their conversation, and refused to leave until Tono excused himself to attend to her. Despite her husband's death, the woman seemed untouched, keeping the same tough exterior as before. However, Brie believed that under that shield of indifference, she must be secretly weeping. Mrs. Nosaka was alone now, and she still had plenty of years ahead.

When Tono returned, he told them, "I have many arrangements to make and must ask you to leave, but I have a favor to ask. Would you join me tonight? There will be a private wake. Before you agree, I must warn you that it will be an all-night affair."

"We would be honored," Sir answered.

"It will be a private ceremony. Later, my family will have an event for his many followers, but tonight my mother and I covet our privacy. Although she is uncomfortable with you being invited, she understands it is important to me and welcomes you to join us."

Brie bowed to him. "Thank you for including us, Tono. Please thank your mother as well."

"I'm grateful to have you with me." He looked at Sir and added, "Both of you."

Sir and Brie spent the day getting themselves prepared for the wake. First, Sir purchased the appropriate clothing, stating that black was the only acceptable attire. He purchased a suit of black, from his jacket and tie to his socks, as well as Brie's modest dress, simple hose and shoes.

Sir explained as he paid for them, "In a sense, we are acting as part of Tono's family. It is important that we fit in as seamlessly as possible."

"Agreed, Sir."

Next he took her to a tiny shop, and purchased a small white envelope with black-and-white ribbon as well as a box of colored pencils. She was curious and asked about the purchases, but Sir told her he would explain later.

When they arrived back at the hotel, he got the ice bucket and set it on the coffee table. Picking up a set of chopsticks, he commanded, "I want to you to practice picking up the pencils and putting them in the container."

She found the task odd, but carefully laid the set of pencils on the table and tried to pick them up with the chopsticks. It wasn't easy, and she dropped many of them in the process, but eventually she transferred all of them safely into the bucket.

He shook his head and stated, "Again."

She looked up at him, chagrined, but dutifully started the process again with only slightly better success.

"Brie, this is important. You must pick up each pencil and gently place it in the container. You cannot drop any of them. Continue with your practice until you are able to do so flawlessly, then summon me so that I may observe it."

He disappeared into the bedroom to use his laptop, leaving Brie to her odd assignment. She knew that this exercise had some bigger meaning, because Sir did not indulge in silly games. Everything he did had a purpose;

everything he asked of her was important and must be mastered.

Sadly, it took hours before she was able to consistently get the pencils from the table to the bucket without mishap. She was bursting with pride when she finally went to him and announced, "I'm ready, Sir."

He looked up from his work and smiled. "Good. Impress me, babygirl." He followed her out to the sitting room and watched with interest as she carefully picked up each pencil and deposited it in the container with care.

"Well done. Were the occasion less melancholy, I would reward you with a session. But given the circumstances, my words of praise must suffice, my dear."

She smiled shyly. "Your praise is always cherished, Sir. May I ask the reason for the task?"

"It will become evident should the need arise. I'm unsure how much we will be involved in the wake and funeral, but it is better to be fully prepared than woefully lacking." He looked at his watch. "It's time to dress. Put your hair up in a modest style, and only use minimal makeup."

They returned to the bedroom together in silence, the mood between them somber as they dressed for the wake. Brie wondered what it would be like and desperately hoped she could be a true comfort to Tono, rather than an unwanted distraction.

A Touching Farewell

They arrived at the Nosaka home just as the sun was setting. Before Brie exited the car, Sir handed her the white envelope, which he'd wrapped in black-and-white ribbon.

"What is this, Sir?"

"It's our *koden*, our condolence money. It's tradition at a wake. A tricky business, too, because giving too much signifies a closer relationship than you have with the deceased, but giving too little is seen as an insult."

"How did you know how much to give, Sir?"

He gave her a playful wink. "I googled it."

They stood behind a group of Tono's family members as they waited for the door to be answered. No one acknowledged them, making Brie extremely grateful when Tono was the one who opened the door. He greeted each person individually before inviting them inside. His calm demeanor and gentle voice belied the fact that his heart was breaking.

Tono's smile was genuine when he saw Brie, but he addressed his greeting to Sir. "Thank you both for joining me tonight."

"We owe you no less, Ren. It's a privilege to be included among your close relatives."

Tono led them to the room that held his father. The body had been packed in dry ice, and a white cloth covered his face. People were already seated on the floor, facing the body. Sir directed Brie to sit at the back, but Tono asked them to join him at the front. Brie knew it must be an unusual request, and was not surprised to hear a protest from his mother.

Tono answered his mother by pointing to Sir and stating simply, "*Ani*" and then gesturing to Brie and saying, "*Imouto*". His mother grunted under her breath, but nodded and put her hands together, bowing to them from where she sat.

"I told her you are like a brother and sister to me," Tono explained.

Brie smiled, and returned his mother's bow before sitting down beside Tono. Being so close to him, she was able to sync her breath to his, and the peace of that connection floated between them.

A Buddhist priest began chanting, and the smell of burning incense filled the room. Many of those in attendance were fingering prayer beads as he spoke. Eventually, the priest gave a signal and the family members closest to the body began to get up, one at a time, offering incense at an altar beside his father's body. When Tono's turn came, he stood up and nodded to Brie, indicating that he wanted her to do the same. Brie watched carefully as he knelt beside the altar, took a pinch of incense and brought it to his forehead before sprinkling it into the flaming bowl. He did this three times and bowed again before sitting back down beside her.

Brie got up and went to the altar, terrified of doing something wrong and offending his extended family in some way. She swallowed down that fear as she knelt gracefully and stared at the picture of Master Nosaka on the altar. While she remembered vividly how cold and hurtful those eyes could be, in this picture he was smiling slightly and his eyes shone with pride.

She took a pinch of the incense and sent a silent message to the man. *Thank you for raising Tono to be such an honorable person.* She sprinkled the incense into the flame and took another pinch. *Thank you for teaching him your skill of Kinbaku.* She let the incense burn and took a final pinch. *And thank you for finding me worthy of your son.* Tears pricked her eyes as she sprinkled the incense into the fire and watched it smoke. She stared at the still body beside her and said with silent conviction, *Although we cannot be together, I promise I will do everything in my power to support your son now and in the future.*

As she bowed one last time, Brie whispered, "Thank you for sharing your talent of singing, too. It is a charming side of you both I never suspected."

When she returned to Tono's side, Sir got up. She watched as he paid his respects. This quiet, reverent ceremony was beautiful in its simplicity. It allowed those who had known the deceased to reflect on memories of him in the safety and warmth of the place he'd called home.

When everyone had offered incense, the priest finished with more chanting. The ceremony ended once he was done, and most of the people in the room left at that time. Brie watched as Tono handed each person a small box before they walked out the door.

She whispered to Sir, "What's he doing?"

"He is giving a thank you gift to them."

An older woman touched Sir's sleeve and gestured that they should follow her. Sir guided Brie down the hallway and into a dining room with a low-lying table laden with food.

Just like in the States, food played a central part when people passed away. Those already seated at the table spoke in quiet tones as they waited for Tono to arrive. Brie discreetly took hold of Sir's hand under the table and squeezed it.

As soon as Tono entered, the level of conversation became livelier. Plates were passed out and people used chopsticks to help themselves to the feast. Brie looked dubiously at the food, realizing that most of what was on the table was seafood—something Brie could not stomach. How could she possibly navigate the meal without offending anyone?

Tono noticed her hesitation and offered several suggestions about what she would find appetizing. He winked, telling her, "As long as you do not put it on your plate, you are not expected to eat it."

She took a rice ball and a little of each food he'd suggested, and settled back to eat it, grateful for Sir's insistence that she practice her chopstick skills at the hotel. It allowed her to observe those at the table now without worrying about embarrassing herself.

Brie found it easy to pick out Master Nosaka's siblings. They all had similar features and the same stoic expression. Despite their serious demeanor, the discussions were animated and several times the entire table broke out in laughter. She desperately wished she knew Japanese so she could savor the stories they were sharing.

She glanced in Mrs. Nosaka's direction. The woman had a cross look on her face, but Brie noticed she was staring off into the distance, as if lost in old memories. If she would have welcomed it, Brie would have given her a hug.

Instead, Brie turned to Tono and asked, "How are you doing tonight?"

He gave a tired sigh. "Still in shock, unable to accept that he's really gone."

He looked thoroughly exhausted and emotionally beaten. "You should get some rest after the meal," she suggested.

Tono snorted, sounding insulted when he replied, "No, tonight we stay up and watch over my father."

Sir replied smoothly, "Of course, Nosaka. Brie was just expressing her concern for you."

Tono nodded in understanding and explained to her, "This is my last night with my father. I gladly give up rest."

After dinner, they went back into the room with his father. One woman was already there, standing beside the body, talking softly. The three of them sat down quietly, so as not to disturb her, with Brie and Sir sitting on either side of Tono.

The sound of the woman's voice was light, as if she was recalling happy memories, but near the end her voice became raw and anguished. Brie couldn't bear her pain and looked down as a tear fell into her lap. She glanced sideways at Tono.

He sat with a rigid back, his eyes focused on his father. Multiple people came to talk with Master Nosaka throughout the night, as if he were still alive, and Brie found it touching. However, Tono never moved; his gaze never wavered.

As dawn approached, the price of his vigilance made itself known when he tried to shake off the exhaustion. Brie got up and whispered to Sir, asking permission before she slipped her hand into Tono's, willing her energy to flow from her into him.

Tono closed his eyes, not outwardly acknowledging the contact, but he held on to her hand tightly. They remained that way until hours later, when his mother beckoned to him to speak with her outside the room.

His movements were stiff as he got up to leave. Tono returned a short time later with a small box in his hand. "Thank you for your company, Sir Davis, Miss Bennett. Please return to your hotel room and rest if you can. We'll meet again at noon. There are things I must take care of before the funeral." He handed Sir a card with directions and gave Brie the gift.

"Can I help in any way?" Sir asked.

"No. This is my honor and duty. Please rest." He bowed to them before leaving the room.

Brie was surprised when they arrived hours later and saw the funeral home swarmed by journalists. "Poor Tono! Why can't they leave his family alone?"

Sir said with a frustrated sigh, "It's unfortunate, but the intrusion must be endured." He opened the car door and held out his hand. "Come, Brie." They ignored the cameras and flurry of questions in English, as they sought to find Tono inside.

To Brie's relief, they found him with his father, whose body had been placed in a casket. She was surprised to see young children in the room. The smell of incense filled the air as the priest spoke and people paid their final respects, leaving flowers in the casket.

Afterwards, the casket was sealed and rolled away with silent reverence. "What's going on, Sir?" Brie whispered as people began filing out of the room.

"They're going to cremate Master Nosaka's body while we wait."

She glanced behind her, shuddering at the thought. It seemed so…final.

Tono joined them, smiling curtly at Brie. Was she the only one who saw the agony behind those chocolate-brown eyes?

"It's a shame the funeral was publicized," Sir told him.

"Yes, it has my mother in an unpleasant state. I reminded her that last night was undisturbed, but it seems to be of little comfort to her now."

The room he led them to was expansive, with plenty of seating and large amounts of food set out for the mourners, but eating was the last thing on Brie's mind. She thought she spotted Chikako across the room and asked Tono, "Is that your partner from the studio?"

"Yes," he answered. "Many people my father worked with are here to pay their respects today. They were like family to *Otosama*, so I invited them to attend the funeral despite my mother's objections. Funerals are meant for the living, not the dead."

"And who are the children?" Brie asked, as a tiny girl with pigtails walked past.

"Part of my father's side of the family."

"You have adorable relatives," Brie complimented, waving to the little girl, who giggled and waved back.

"Please partake of the food while I defuse the confrontation about to take place," Tono growled under his breath, heading towards his mother.

Brie wasn't interested in eating, so she watched the other people in the room, wondering what their stories were and what role they had played in Tono's life. One thing that struck her was the respect they all showed to Tono. It was gratifying to see.

After he'd neutralized the situation, Tono disappeared from the room.

"Brie, go after him," Sir commanded. "He's almost at his breaking point."

She hurried out to the hallway and followed it down until she found Tono leaning against a wall, his eyes closed—the pain he suffered rolling off him in tangible waves.

"Tono," she whispered as she approached.

He opened his eyes, shaking his head. "I'm not strong enough for this."

"Then you can lean on me today," she offered.

He laughed miserably. "Today I can handle. It's the countless days ahead I can't face."

Brie felt certain that once he was far from his mother, he would regain his peace. "How much longer do you plan on staying, Tono?"

"You don't understand, do you? As the only child, it is my duty to care for my mother."

"But you can't," Brie protested. "It will crush your spirit to remain here with her."

He closed his eyes again. "The moment I realized that my father was dying, I knew what lay ahead for me. This is *not* the life I wanted, but it is the one I must live out."

Tono smiled down at her sadly. "The only consolation I have is that by not collaring you, I did not make this your fate as well."

"Oh, Tono…"

He said with certainty, "It's better this way. I understand that now."

"But I don't want this for you!" Brie cried.

Tono took her forcefully by the shoulders. "What I *need* is your understanding and support."

Brie bit her lip and nodded. "You have my unwavering support, Tono. You always will."

"Good," he said, releasing his hold on her. "Then go back home and start on your new film. It would bring me joy to see your career grow. Make me proud, Brie."

Tears of love and gratitude ran down her cheeks as she hugged him. "I don't want to leave you."

"But you must."

He guided her back to the gathering in silence.

When they arrived, the attendant was directing people to a new room. Brie left Tono's side as he helped to escort his relatives out of the room. She made her way through the crowd to rejoin Sir.

"How did it go?" he asked.

She wiped away the remnants of her tears. "He's staying in Japan, Sir."

"I assumed he would." As they followed behind the large party, Sir told her, "Keep an open mind, Brie. The Japanese culture holds many meaningful rituals we're unfamiliar with in the West."

She thought he was talking about Tono's choice to stay, but realized he wasn't as soon as she entered the new room. She paused for a moment, taken aback.

Brie stared down at the white ashes of Tono's father, and tears came to her eyes.

"As acting members of Tono's family," Sir explained, "we will be helping to separate his bones from the ashes." A gold tray lay across the middle of the receptacle that held the ashes. On it sat a beautifully decorated urn, one Brie was certain Tono had painted himself.

As she watched, the family members began reverently picking up bone fragments with special chopsticks and placing them into the urn.

"Come, Brie," Sir commanded, handing her a set of the chopsticks. She steadied her hand as she stood beside Tono and helped in the ritual, silently thanking Sir for his earlier lesson.

Tono nodded his approval as she carefully deposited a piece of bone into the urn.

Everyone participated, even the children, as the family made sure Master Nosaka's remains were lovingly retrieved and put in the vessel. Afterwards, the lid was placed on the urn and handed to Tono.

His mother grabbed it from him and held it to her chest, her fingers turning white from her deathlike grip on it—the first outward sign of her grief.

Tono escorted his mother through the crush of reporters and took her to his car, but before he drove off he came back to Brie and Sir.

"I will never forget the honor you paid my father today."

"It was not only for him, Nosaka."

Tono bowed to Sir. "*Domo.*"

Brie was surprised when Tono suddenly embraced Sir. The two men hugged each other, both familiar with the grief of losing their fathers.

"May I?" Tono asked him afterwards, turning to Brie.

"Certainly, Ren."

Tono took Brie in his arms and held her tenderly for several moments before the obnoxious clicking of the cameras became too much. "Thank you," he whispered when he let her go.

Brie's eyes watered as Tono drove away. So much grief and hardship faced him in the weeks and months ahead.

"He'll be fine, Brie."

"I hope so, Sir."

"I guarantee it. In all my life, I've never met a stronger man."

Denver-Bound

B rie was emotionally and physically spent after the funeral, and collapsed on the hotel bed. But the gift Tono had given them at the wake caught her eye. She heeded its call and pulled herself off the bed to retrieve the white box.

Untying the jute binding, Brie smiled when she found a perfect white orchid inside. It had been painted in some kind of hard preserving material so that the flower remained looking as fresh as the day it'd been picked. The exquisite blossom was attached to a silver comb.

Sir took it from her and placed it in her hair. "It looks beautiful on you."

Brie lightly fingered the flower and smiled. "I'll wear it whenever I film."

"An excellent plan. Although I have a few more days left here, I think it would be best for you to return to the States to begin your documentary."

"But Sir…"

He shook his head. "You have done all you can for

Nosaka. It's time to honor his request."

"But we didn't get to say goodbye," she whimpered.

"Yesterday was his farewell, Brie."

Her heart sank when she realized Sir was right.

"Return to the US and write him letters sharing details about your filming. *That* is how you will help to support Nosaka through this."

She understood, but her heart was breaking just the same.

Sir chuckled kindly, caressing her cheek. "Every emotion plays out on your face. I love that about you, téa." He kissed her on the lips slowly, tenderly.

Brie gave in to the magic of his touch as he carefully took out the comb and laid it on the table.

"Let me make love to you before we say goodbye," he said, pushing her gently onto the bed. "Death has a way of helping you to appreciate what you have."

She closed her eyes as he undid the buttons on her blouse and moved the material aside to stare at her chest. He kissed the round swell of her breast before returning to her lips.

"Right now, all that exists is you, me and this moment in time."

She opened her eyes and nodded, lifting her lips to meet his.

Sir's lovemaking was unusually gentle and sweet. Light, lingering kisses and soft, teasing caresses carried her to heavenly release...

Later that night, he printed out her plane tickets and handed them over to her. "In just a few hours, you'll be Denver-bound."

Denver? She looked down at her ticket to confirm she'd heard him correctly.

"I think a trip to Master Anderson's new Training Center will prove quite helpful for your new film."

"Oh, my gosh, I'll get to see Lea!"

Sir smiled. "I can just imagine the giggles now."

Brie threw her arms around him. "Thank you, Sir. This is exactly what I needed!"

He chuckled warmly, returning her embrace. "I'll join you when I'm done here. I'm curious myself to see how their new Center is faring." Brie wondered if Sir wanted to personally check up on Ms. Clark, as well.

"I'll get to see Baron, too! Maybe even do a little sightseeing while I'm there," she squealed.

"Take it all in, Brie," he encouraged, lightly grazing her lips with his finger.

"Does anyone know I'm coming?"

He said with a smirk, "Only Brad."

"Eek! I can't wait to see the look on Lea's face when I show up."

"Yes, I believe Anderson has a little something planned for your reunion with her. I look forward to hearing about it."

Brie grinned at her tickets, before attacking Sir with a flurry of kisses.

Ready or not, Denver, here I come...

A Slave's Dream

S he had been called to join Master Anderson in room eighteen. Although it was highly unusual to meet after school hours, Sir had assured her the lesson was essential if she wanted to graduate from the Center.

Brie had been working hard for nearly six weeks— *nothing* was going to stand in the way of her making it to Graduation Night. She hurried through the familiar hallways, awkwardly sprinting in her six-inch heels to make it to her class on time.

She opened the door and froze for a second. Master Anderson was tightly gripping the bullwhip in his hand. She'd already felt its bite at The Haven and didn't want to relive the experience.

"Come in, young Brie."

She walked hesitantly over the threshold and took off her blouse and bra with shaking fingers. She knelt down, putting her hands behind her back in the position Sir had instructed she take upon entering a room with a trainer.

Her heart rate shot up as she listened to his boots

echoing in the large room as he approached. Master Anderson put his hand on her head and stated in a sultry voice, "Stand and serve me well, slave."

Her stomach did a flip-flop when he called her 'slave'. She gracefully rocked off her heels and stood before him. "It would be my honor, Master Anderson."

"You will call me only Master tonight."

She bowed her head in acknowledgement of his command, but her heart fluttered. Calling him Master had a completely different feel to it, especially since she was to be his slave for the session.

"Master, what is the focus of tonight's lesson?"

"We are going to test your willingness to please in the face of challenge."

Brie sucked in her breath. This did not sound as if it was going to be an easy lesson—a part of her wanted to bolt from the room, but she'd come too far to give up now.

"Challenge me, Master," she stated confidently.

"Stand on the X to receive my pleasure."

Brie shivered as she made her way to the brightly painted red X on the floor. The skin on her back tingled in anticipation, knowing the sensations she was about to experience.

"Hands up, slave."

She lifted her arms and he secured her trembling wrists in the leather cuffs attached to overhanging chains. The clinking sound of the metal announced that there was no escape for her.

Brie heard the door open as another set of footsteps announced someone else had entered the room. She felt a commanding presence behind her, then a familiar deep, baritone voice asked, "Is she ready for me?"

Her breath caught and that old feeling of fear mixed with expectation washed over her. *Was* she ready for Baron?

"Undress her," Master Anderson stated.

Brie felt the dark Dom's strong hands caress her small waist before he unzipped her skirt and let it fall to the floor. She held her breath when his lips landed on her neck as he slipped off her lace panties.

Once she was naked, he wrapped his strong hands around her hip bones and pressed his hardening cock against her. "You will be well used tonight, kitten."

Brie let out a ragged gasp when Baron bit down on her neck before releasing her.

She swayed in the chains, unsure whether she could handle the lesson the two Doms had planned for her. Baron moved her long hair forward so it swished against her erect nipples, while he whispered in her ear, "I must make the path clear…."

Brie shivered when he moved away, knowing her skin would soon feel the fiery bite of Master Anderson's bullwhip. Without meaning to, she whimpered.

"Are you scared, slave?" Master Anderson asked.

It would be foolish to lie to her trainer, so she answered clearly, "I am, Master."

She heard him warm up as he cracked the whip behind her. She unintentionally stiffened in response to the intimidating sound. "Relax…" he encouraged just as the whip flicked across her back, licking her skin with its light caress.

Brie had forgotten how sweet the bullwhip could be and purred in pleasure, closing her eyes to take in the gentle strokes applied by Master Anderson's skillful hand. After several minutes of light play he stopped, and Baron approached again, gliding his fingers over her womanly curves, concentrating his efforts on her sensitive breasts.

"Your body begs to be played with." Baron rolled her nipples between his fingers, causing her to moan as waves of heat traveled down to her loins. She squirmed on the red X, the chains clinking with every slight movement.

Baron shifted around to face her. He lifted Brie's chin and kissed her with those delicious full lips. She groaned this time, her pussy already wet, preparing itself for the impending coupling.

His sensual lips slowly traveled from her mouth to her chin, farther down her throat until they landed on her left nipple. He suckled it, sending ripples of pleasure through her.

Brie moaned when she felt Master Anderson come up behind, his need obvious as his cock settled between her butt cheeks. "Slave, you will take my challenging strokes, then you will service both your Doms."

"At the same time, Master?" she asked breathlessly as Baron continued to consume her with his hungry kisses.

"Naturally, slave."

Brie's knees buckled when she heard his answer for she knew how well-endowed Master Anderson was.

He chuckled as he slipped his hand between her legs and pressed his fingers against her mound as he lifted her back to her feet. "You can feign resistance, but this pussy tells me otherwise."

Swirling his fingers over her wet clit, Master Anderson then slowly pressed three of them against her opening. With his massive cock still wedged between the cheeks of her ass, he commanded, "Push against my fingers. Force them inside you."

Brie moaned with desire as she strove to obey his command. Baron switched to her other nipple as she leaned harder on Master Anderson's hand, the width of all three fingers stretching her inner lips.

"Good slave. Show your Master how desperate you are to be fucked by two men."

She started to grind against him, begging, "Your slave *needs* to be used for pleasure, Master."

He slowly thrust his fingers while Baron ravished her breasts with his talented mouth. The aggressive attention of both men was incredibly hot and had her pussy aching with need.

Without warning, the two pulled away. She cried out, desperate for their continued caresses.

"Ready yourself, slave," Master Anderson stated, snapping the bullwhip. "The next cry you make will come because of my lash."

Her burning need for them overcame her fear of the whip and she dutifully steeled herself for his onslaught. She shifted in the chains, forcing her muscles to relax.

"Isn't she beautiful like this?" Master Anderson asked Baron. "Totally helpless and afraid, yet completely willing."

"Yes—as stunning as she is bound, it's her enthusiasm for what is about to come that makes my cock ache for her."

Brie smiled, coveting the praise of both Doms.

"Open your legs wider," Master Anderson commanded.

Brie spread her legs farther, which forced her to tiptoe to keep that position. She could only imagine the erotic pose it presented to the men. Although it was challenging, it made her that much more focused and attentive.

"This will bite, slave," Master Anderson warned her as the first stroke exploded across her skin. Brie held her cry to a whimper as she swayed from the impact. The burning sensation radiated over her entire back. The second lash was just as intense, taking her breath away. She concentrated on the fire, not resisting its burn.

Master Anderson took his time, pausing between pairings. The third and fourth lashes challenged her, but by the fifth she'd started to fly.

She squeaked when she felt Baron's warm tongue licking her moist sex below. He shouldn't be there with Master Anderson still whipping her back, and she looked down in surprise, moaning when he grabbed her buttocks, burying his face in her mound.

Brie relaxed and allowed his tongue to possess her, assuming the bullwhip session had ended. She screamed out in unexpected ecstasy when another slash across her skin caused a fiery burst that rushed straight to her groin.

The next stroke of Master Anderson's whip brought on an orgasm that Baron rode with his tongue. Brie cried as reality blurred, mingling with the dual sensations. She was finally experiencing that elusive state she'd longed for—floating between the balance of passion and exquisite pain.

When they eventually stopped, Baron moved her legs together so she could stand comfortably, but she hung from the chains, her whole body weak from their intense play.

Master Anderson's rough hands caressed her sweaty shoulders, then he lightly traced the welts he had created on her back. Gently wiping the tears from Brie's face, he murmured his comfort and praise. When his lips landed firmly on hers, the demanding kiss awakened her inner animal. She growled, her tongue becoming aggressive as she explored Master Anderson's mouth.

He grabbed her head with both hands and kissed her harder, inciting a greater need to be satisfied. Brie's mind swirled with insatiable desire and she bit his bottom lip when he tried to pull away. Master Anderson slapped her ass hard, chuckling as he slowly unbuckled her wrists from the cuffs. She collapsed into Baron's waiting arms and was carried to a bed on the other side of the room.

Baron laid her down carefully, then proceeded to undress before her. His glistening dark skin, rigid shaft and masculine scent called to her and she reached out to him. "I need you."

His response was to flash a mischievous smile. "Not yet, kitten."

Brie glanced over and saw Master Anderson cleaning his whip. Her pussy contracted when he looked in her direction. The lust in those green eyes captivated her. She stared into them like a frightened deer that knew it was about to be devoured—and oh, how she wanted to be devoured by him.

As he walked towards her, Master Anderson stripped off his shirt then unlatched his belt, dropping it to the floor. By the time he reached the edge of the bed, he'd already unzipped his pants to reveal his massive shaft. "Now that we have you loosened up, we will show you no mercy, slave."

"No mercy," she agreed, licking her lips in anticipation.

Brie's breath came in quick gasps as she watched the men lubricate their cocks. Baron's shaft was dark, handsome and thick, while Master Anderson's was ruddy, and branchlike in its length and circumference—a challenging cock for any woman. To take both seemed impossible for her small frame.

Master Anderson wiped his hands before joining her on the bed. He lay on his back and commanded lustfully, "Force my cock inside you, slave."

Brie was slow to straddle him, still a bit shaky from her sub-high. She raised herself over his impressive shaft and, with his support, lowered herself onto it. Initially her body resisted his girth. She bit her lip as she pressed against the head of his enormous shaft, refusing to fail this lesson. Her pussy lips stretched out achingly as his manhood finally slid into her.

Brie gasped as Master Anderson's manhood filled her, but she smiled triumphantly at him once she'd settled fully onto it. He gripped her waist and lifted her up, letting her slowly descend back down. She continued the slow dance, enthralled by the fire it created between them.

"Are you ready for me?" Baron said in a slow drawl, stroking his shaft as he watched.

For the first time Brie felt a twinge of fear, but the thought of pushing her body to the ultimate limit was actually exciting for her. She moaned when she felt the bed shift as Baron made his way to her.

Caressing her ass, he commented, "I've never had the opportunity to enjoy this part of you." Baron gently coated her tight hole with extra lubricant and began to massage her rosette, slowly pushing his finger inside her. She closed her eyes, her whole body tingling at the thought of his thick shaft claiming her.

"Slave."

Brie opened her eyes and stared into Master Anderson's intense, jade-colored ones. His lustful need demanded she satiate it.

"Hold yourself open for him."

She obediently lay her torso on Master Anderson's broad chest and put her arms behind her, spreading herself open for Baron. It added an element of exposure and vulnerability.

"Kitten…" Baron growled as he pressed his cock against her resistant opening. She expected he would force himself in, but he seemed to be waiting.

Brie looked back questioningly.

"That's it, kitten, look at me."

Brie whimpered as the roundness of his thick head pressed hard against her. Taking his full circumference seemed unachievable, but after several minutes of gentle thrusts, her taut muscles relaxed enough to draw him inside.

Both men groaned.

She started to pant heavily as Baron rocked his shaft deeper into her. Master Anderson told her to prop herself up on his chest so he could play with her breasts. As soon as his hands began to tug and pull on her nipples, her body's resistance eased, allowing the manly invasion.

Master Anderson grabbed her buttocks while Baron wrapped his hands around her waist and both men began to thrust at the same time. Brie cried out, her whole body shuddering from the deep ache it caused. It took everything in her to accept the movement of both shafts, but she willingly gave herself to the sensation, begging them to take her deeper.

"Slave," Master Anderson called as she started to fly from their dual attention. She resisted his call, wanting to get lost in the feeling of complete surrender. "Slave," he insisted.

Brie reluctantly opened her eyes, looking at him in confusion when he instructed, "Return your seats to an upright position and keep your seatbelts fastened until we are parked safely at the gate."

Brie woke with a start, and found herself gazing into the questioning eyes of her seatmate on the plane.

"Good dream?" the middle-aged woman asked with obvious amusement.

Mistress Isa

Brie smiled self-consciously as she stared out the airplane window at the snow-capped mountains, while the plane slowly pulled up to the gate. She'd always pictured Denver being closer to the Rocky Mountains, but that didn't seem to be the case at all. It was more like a sprawling city on the flat plains, with the mountains acting as a magnificent backdrop.

She would have been disappointed, but the fact that Lea lived here made Denver a magical place. Brie longed to see the look on her best friend's face when she surprised her. Sir had mentioned that Master Anderson had something special in mind for their initial meeting. Brie couldn't begin to guess what it might be, however she trusted it would prove entertaining.

Master Anderson was the kind of Dom who could make you laugh one instant and bring you to your knees the next.

When the plane came to a complete stop, Brie pulled her cell phone from her purse and texted him, a hint of a blush coloring her cheeks as she thought back on her dream.

I'm here!

She glanced nervously at her phone when she exited the airport train. Master Anderson had yet to respond to her text and Sir hadn't given her any instructions other than to meet the Dom once she landed. She had no idea where Master Anderson might be and wasn't allowed to call Lea to find out.

Brie headed up the escalator to the main terminal and looked around anxiously. There was a crowd of people waiting to greet loved ones coming off the train. Out of curiosity, she scanned the signs the limo drivers held up and was surprised to see the name "Young Brie". Her eyes trailed from the sign to the face of the man holding it. She grinned when she saw Master Anderson, who happened to be looking damn sexy in the cowboy hat he was wearing.

She ran up to him, giggling when he lifted her into the air and twirled her around. When he set her back on the ground, he tipped his hat. "Good to see you again, young Brie."

Brie gazed at him bashfully, taken in by his leather boots, tight jeans and plaid shirt unbuttoned just enough to show off his muscular chest. "I never suspected you were a cowboy, Mast—Mr. Anderson."

He winked at her. "Grew up in Greely but outgrew my cowboy ways by college. Now I only dress this way to welcome friends to the Mile High City." He leaned down. "I've noticed it seems to fluster women, and if my eyes don't deceive me, I do believe there's a rosy blush on those cheeks."

Brie looked away, turning a deeper shade of red as images of her naughty dream resurfaced. Master Anderson had no idea…

"Come with me," he said, holding out his elbow. She smiled as she took his arm, quite aware of the slew of women openly ogling him as they made their way to the baggage claim area. She snuck a glance at him as they waited for her luggage to arrive. Yep, her old trainer looked quite devastating in that black cowboy hat.

To avoid further wicked thoughts, she asked him, "Did you learn your skills with the bullwhip as a little boy in Greely, then?"

When he grinned down at her, Brie heard a woman beside her murmur to herself, "Yum…" It made Brie giggle. Master Anderson was quite the charmer.

"Yes, I played around with it while my father was off herding cattle. Rather humorous and painful sessions, as I recall. I was small and couldn't handle the whip's length. Even then, however, it felt like an extension of myself—my calling, so to speak."

Brie blushed again, remembering her session with him at The Haven. "I agree that it's your calling, Mr. Anderson. You are very skil—"

"Pardon me," the woman behind her interrupted. She twirled her bleached blonde hair in a flirtatious manner when she asked, "Are you a famous bull rider or something?"

Master Anderson laughed. "I am not."

"So no chance I'll be seeing you at the State Fair this year?"

"No, my time is taken up wrangling young heifers

with my whip."

"Oooh…" the young woman squealed. "I like the sound of that. Maybe I can watch you sometime?"

Master Anderson tipped his hat before grabbing Brie's luggage from the carousel. "I believe my style of wrangling would alarm you, miss. Better you chase those bull riders at the rodeo."

She pouted as Master Anderson guided Brie out of the airport.

Once they left the building and were safe from being overheard, Brie admitted, "I fully expected you to invite her to your new training center."

He raised his eyebrow. "That young woman? She's not submissive material."

"Really? How can you tell?"

"There's a gut feeling whenever I interact with women." Master Anderson threw her luggage into the back of his Chevy truck and opened the door for her. "Plus the fact she interrupted you to flirt with me. Submissives tend not to be overly aggressive—and most have much better manners."

It turned out the drive to his new training center was a long one, since the airport was east of the city and Master Anderson's training center was southwest of it, nestled against the foothills. While he navigated through heavy traffic, Master Anderson explained his elaborate plan to surprise Lea—but it wasn't just her best friend his little stunt would involve.

Brie protested after he'd finished explaining it to her, "Ms. Clark is going to hate me even more than she already does."

"For your information, Samantha is far less uptight these days."

Master Anderson added curtly, "Besides, your Master told you to obey me in this. Regardless of the consequences, I expect full cooperation from you."

The Dom had effectively put her in her place, and she bowed her head. "Yes, Master Anderson."

He chuckled to himself, "Oh, young Brie, the fun I have planned this week..." His obvious mirth delighted Brie. Truly, pleasing him would be worth the wrath of the infamous Ms. Clark.

Brie was excited as the magnificent peaks loomed ever closer on their drive, but he surprised her by not going straight to his training center. Instead Master Anderson took her to an upscale community in the mountainous valley just west of the city. It looked like an exclusive neighborhood—the kind that comprised the elite of Denver society.

He pulled into a long driveway that led up to a ranch-style home. The natural color of the house blended well with the environment around it. It was unique in its rustic style compared to the fancier homes in the area.

He sighed deeply as he stared at his house. "I had to give up my old Victorian in town. After purchasing the building for my Academy, I found the daily commute unbearable. Fortunately, by giving up the historical charm of my old place, I no longer have to fight traffic and I now get to enjoy this fantastic view."

Brie got out of the car and admired the scenic foothills surrounding them. He was right, the view was truly impressive. She took in a deep breath and swore the mountain air seemed lighter, more vibrant. "I can definitely see why you like it here."

"Glad you approve."

Master Anderson proudly escorted her into his home. It turned out to be equally impressive. The main room had tall ceilings and large windows showcasing his immaculate backyard. Before she had a chance to take it all in, he pointed to the first door on the right. "You'll find your outfit on the bed."

Brie was curious what he had picked out, and laughed out loud when she saw her costume. She called from the bedroom, "You can't be serious."

His deep voice answered, "I'm quite serious."

After donning the long-sleeved tunic with an over-sized hood, she looked in the mirror and shook her head. "I look like Obi-Wan Kenobi."

Brie walked out of the room and sat down on a leather couch, waiting for Master Anderson to join her. To the left was a well-equipped kitchen, with even more gadgets and doodads than his home in California.

The great room sported a massive stone fireplace. Instead of family photos decorating his mantel, there was a kayak mounted high on the wall, complete with two wooden oars.

Her eyes were drawn to the greenery of the backyard just beyond. It had a large fence lined with young trees and bushes. Most notable, however, was the wooden pole in the center. Brie knew it was used for bullwhip practice and wondered what his new neighbors thought about the oddly placed post.

Master Anderson came out a short time later, looking

refined and businesslike in a tailored gray suit.

"Why the change of dress?" Brie asked, standing as he entered the room.

"A very important person from the Orient is coming to the Academy of Denver today. Naturally I would dress up for such a prestigious individual."

"I can't believe you are making me do this," she groaned.

He grabbed her chin. "One hundred percent commitment, young Brie. When you walk in, I want them to feel your dominance. No…make it arrogance. You *are* Mistress Isa, highly respected Dominatrix from China."

In response to his command, she removed his hand from her wrist and lifted her chin defiantly. "Do not touch me—I am your equal."

He smiled but corrected her. "No, my dear, you are my superior. I cannot equal your expertise, which is why you have been invited to join us at the Academy."

She sighed nervously; this was so far out of her comfort zone.

"No more sighs, Mistress Isa."

"No more sighs," she agreed.

As Brie got up, she began to mentally embrace her role. She strode past Master Anderson with an air of supremacy as she left the house. She waited beside the truck, going over in her mind the persona she was taking on.

She was a Mistress from China, renowned for her use of acupuncture during BDSM play. Having an adventurous spirit and a natural curiosity about American culture, she'd come to Colorado at the invitation of

Master Anderson. She was not intimidated by others because she knew her skills were unparalleled. Doms and subs alike showed her the respect she was due. Her odd tunic had a purpose. It hid her identity until she was ready to reveal it—it left her in control.

As Brie belted herself in, she noted how incongruous Master Anderson looked in a business suit, driving his huge truck. "Master Anderson, if you don't consider yourself a cowboy, why do you drive this vehicle?"

He smirked. "No matter how much I deny it, you can't take the cowboy out of the man."

He drove her fifteen minutes away, to a large building that looked like a giant warehouse. It was not at all what she had been expecting.

"This is your training center?"

"This is the Academy of Denver," he answered.

"It's so…huge."

"I will have you know a converted home improvement depot is *the* ideal training facility, especially for the practice of bullwhips. High ceilings and large open spaces make the optimal environment. The vast warehouse also leaves plenty of room for future expansion."

"I see, Master Anderson. I meant no offense."

"None taken, young Brie." His eyes sparkled with a mischievous glint. "Now let's have a little fun with my staff."

Brie's heart raced at the thought of seeing Lea again, but she needed to maintain an outer countenance of calm. Master Anderson leaned over and placed the hood over her head so her face was obscured by the ample amount of material. "They'll never see this coming…"

He walked her into the facility, where they were greeted by the receptionist, who struck Brie as both professional and assertive in her sharp business suit.

"Hello, Mistress Isa. It is an honor to meet you."

Brie just nodded in response, as Master Anderson had instructed her to.

"Are all the staff present, Lisa?" Master Anderson asked.

"Yes, Master Anderson. They are waiting for you in the conference room."

"Fine. Oh, and call Adam at the Masters at Arms Club. Let him know I'd like to talk to him about an upcoming charity event."

"Certainly, Master Anderson. What time works best for you to meet?"

"Better make it next week. I want to set time aside so I can introduce Mistress Isa to the many charms of Denver."

"Wonderful." Lisa addressed Brie again. "I hope you will find our city to your liking, Mistress Isa."

Brie gave the slightest of nods and turned from her. It grated on her nerves not to respond with a bow and a thank you, but she was determined to maintain the mystery and poise of Mistress Isa.

Master Anderson explained as they walked, "I want you to wait near the doorway until I come out to get you."

"Naturally I would not enter a room unescorted," she answered, with a coy smile he could not see.

"Nice," he complimented. "That's the attitude I was hoping for."

Master Anderson left her then, joining his staff. The first voice she heard was that of Ms. Clark.

"Is she here? Why didn't you show her in?"

"Calm yourself, Samantha. I wanted to talk to you all first."

"Pardon me," she answered curtly, "but I've been looking forward to meeting Mistress Isa and hate to think of her waiting unnecessarily." Ms. Clark added with just a hint of fangirling in her voice, "To add various stimuli only acupuncture can provide during a scene… I've never had that kind of power. The possibilities are endless."

"I expect her expertise will give our training facility an edge over others in the area. Therefore I've decided to make major changes to the current team."

"What kind of changes?" Ms. Clark asked, suddenly sounding alarmed.

"While some of you may struggle with my decision, keep in mind we are extremely fortunate that Mistress Isa has agreed to join the Academy."

Brie giggled softly to herself.

Baron's rich voice filled the room. "I'm sure I'll be fine with whatever you've decided."

"Agreed!" Lea piped up.

Brie had to hold in the squeal of joy that threatened to escape her lips when she heard Lea's voice.

"Because she has such extensive knowledge and expertise in many areas, I've asked her to lead the Academy. Think of me as more of an overseer for the training facility."

"You're making her Headmistress of the school?"

Ms. Clark asked in disbelief.

"Precisely. She will run the program while I run the business side of things."

"But—"

Baron interrupted. "If Master Anderson is confident she will lead us well, I have no issue with the change in leadership."

"But…" Ms. Clark stammered, "We haven't even met her yet. Being Headmistress is so much more than being an expert at training submissives."

"I understand that, Samantha, and I'm telling you that she is the one I want running the Academy."

Lea spoke up. "Will she have authority over the submissive staff as well, Master Anderson?"

"Yes."

"Like Baron, I trust your judgment and look forward to serving under her," Lea replied amiably.

Ms. Clark was forthright in her response to Master Anderson's announcement. "While I'm humbled to have such a talented Dominatrix included in our organization, I'm a little stunned you're giving up your Headmaster position."

"Mistress Isa is *that* good," Master Anderson assured her.

"Having two Doms and two Dommes on the panel should prove interesting," Baron stated, sounding either intrigued or amused by the thought—Brie couldn't tell which.

"I do understand your concerns, Samantha," Master Anderson said, "so let me be equally frank. Do you think you can work under another woman?"

Ms. Clark took a moment to answer. "Although I do not care for the leadership of other women, Mistress Isa's unique talent and your confidence in her have weight with me. I will find a way to make it work."

"Very good, but a word to the wise—she will not speak or reveal herself unless she finds you worthy. First impressions matter greatly to her."

"I feel as if I'm about to meet royalty," Lea giggled.

Brie heard Master Anderson's footsteps heading towards the door. He stopped midway and stated, "Oh, and another thing—she cannot tolerate others staring her in the eye—especially women." Brie had to cover her mouth to keep from laughing.

A feeling of lightheadedness hit her when Master Anderson emerged from the room to retrieve her. What she was about to do was absolutely crazy!

"Are you ready, Mistress Isa?" he asked with a smirk.

Brie's eagerness to see Lea overcame her misgivings, and she nodded under the massive hood.

"Good." He leaned down and whispered, "Tease them a little before you reveal yourself."

Brie walked into the room, feeling their eyes on her as she glided across the floor to stand before them. *I am your Mistress*, she thought to herself.

"Mistress Isa, this is my staff. To the right is Baron. He is my right-hand man, so to speak."

"It is a pleasure to meet you, Mistress Isa," Baron replied, his voice drawing her in with its deep, rich tone. Brie nodded once.

"Ms. Clark is seated next to him. She was a part of the training staff at the Submissive Training Center in

California for many years and has graciously agreed to act as such for my facility."

Brie peeked up to see whether Ms. Clark was looking at her. To her delight, the trainer held her gaze down when she spoke. "We are grateful to have you join us, Mistress Isa."

Brie took a longer time to nod—just to make Ms. Clark sweat a little.

"Lastly, I have Ms. Taylor. She is the leader of the submissives who will be helping to train Dominants. Our staff is small at this point, but we have plans to expand as the program grows."

Lea got up and moved over to Brie, giving her a proper bow. "Your reputation precedes you, Mistress Isa. Welcome."

Brie grinned as she placed her hand on Lea's head. There was no fear that Lea would look up and notice who really was under the hood, because her friend was a well-trained submissive. When Brie took her hand away, Lea kept her eyes to the floor as she gracefully returned to her seat.

Brie suddenly got a wild hair up her ass and pointed towards Ms. Clark.

It was clear by the silence that followed that the Domme had no idea what to say or do.

Master Anderson encouraged her, "Mistress Isa would like you to speak."

"Certainly…" Ms. Clark replied, pausing as she tried to figure out what Brie wanted. To have that kind of power over someone else was dangerously exhilarating.

"Well, as Master Anderson mentioned, I was a trainer at the Submissive Training Center. I'd like to note that I was the first woman on the panel and my influence led the Dominant training team at the Center to add a woman to their staff as well."

Brie shrugged as if that meant nothing to her, but she knew she would pay a heavy price for putting Ms. Clark in this position despite the fact Master Anderson put her up to it.

Ms. Clark forged onward. "I enjoy working with both male and female submissives and have spent time under a Dominatrix to expand my knowledge."

Brie said nothing, but waved her hand, gesturing that she wanted to hear more.

It was obvious by the slight timbre of her voice that Ms. Clark was flustered. "I look forward to learning your expertise in acupuncture as well. The idea of using Eastern knowledge to enhance BDSM play fascinates me."

"As it should," Brie said in a deep, alluring voice.

"I trust you will impart the techniques you employ to the staff," Ms. Clark added hopefully.

"No."

Ms. Clark gasped softly but said nothing.

Brie was *so* going to pay for this little ruse, but she couldn't help herself. She prayed Master Anderson would protect her from Ms. Clark's justified wrath. She turned to face Baron, still keeping her voice low. "However, you I will teach."

Ms. Clark looked up, an expression of disbelief on her face. The room was uncomfortably silent but Brie could feel Master Anderson's amusement radiating from the man. Brie hoped he would earn Ms. Clark's caning—not she.

Baron replied, "Surely, Mistress Isa, it would be best if the entire staff were familiar with your skills."

"I agree," Master Anderson stated. "Mistress Isa, would you consider demonstrating them on our sub, Ms. Taylor, right now?"

Brie paused, pretending to ponder his request. She knew Lea didn't care for needles, and giggled to herself when she saw her friend twitch in her seat. Master Anderson was delightfully evil on so many levels, but she had something even better in mind.

"Come," she commanded, gesturing to Ms. Clark instead.

From under the hood she watched the trainer's stunned face. Ms. Clark looked to Master Anderson.

He walked over to her and Brie could hear him whisper in the trainer's ear, "This is a good sign, Samantha. She approves of you."

Ms. Clark didn't hesitate. She stood and walked over to Brie. "Please enlighten us, Mistress Isa."

Brie nodded. "As you wish…"

She threw back her hood and grinned at everyone.

Ms. Clark stared at her in shock, as Lea jumped up from her seat and ran over with her arms outstretched.

"It's my Brie!"

Bad Joke

The two girls hugged as Baron slowly clapped his hands. "Well played."

Lea squeezed Brie tight, smothering her with her large bosom. "Oh, my gosh, I can't believe you're really here!"

Brie giggled, disengaging herself in order to catch her breath. "Here in the flesh, girlfriend!"

"Miss Bennett."

"Master Anderson made me do it," Brie blurted, fully expecting to face Ms. Clark's harsh glare, but instead she swore there was a twinkle in the Domme's eyes. It threw her off and she smiled tentatively at the trainer.

Ms. Clark turned to Master Anderson. "I need to stop trusting you. Naturally, I had my doubts when you said Mistress Isa was coming to join the Academy, so I researched her online and found a whole website devoted to the Dominatrix. Based on that, I had to assume she was an actual person."

Master Anderson grinned like a naughty schoolboy. "I did have fun setting that little baby up. Gratifying to know you actually visited the site."

"As did I," Baron replied. "What else would you expect from your training staff?"

Master Anderson threw back his head and laughed. "God, I love running this Academy!"

"If you weren't Headmaster, I would lock you in the stockades," Ms. Clark grumbled, but it was easy to tell she found his prank amusing. She turned her attention back to Brie and Lea. "It appears at least one person is happy to see you, Miss Bennett."

"Yes, it does." Brie gave Lea an extra-hard squeeze and smiled at Ms. Clark, shocked she'd gotten off so easily with the trainer. Would she be made to pay later?

Baron stood from the table and walked over to the group. "It is good to see you again, kitten."

Brie let go of Lea and gave him a hug, resting her head against his broad chest. There'd always been something comforting about the dark Dom—he was her safe place—and she inhaled deeply, taking in his spicy scent.

"How is Sir Davis?"

She broke the embrace and smiled up at him. "He is doing well. Finishing up some business in Japan then joining me here."

"And Tono Nosaka?"

Brie kept it positive, knowing it was what Tono wanted—*needed*—from her. "He's deeply saddened by the loss of his father, but Tono is determined to care for his mother and make the best of a difficult situation."

"That is good to hear," Baron replied in his low, soothing voice. "Tono Nosaka is someone I admire."

"Me too." Brie grinned and hugged him again. "It's just so good to see you again. I've missed you, Baron."

His thick lips curled up in a sexy smirk. "So you miss the old Baron, do you?"

"Of course! Not only did you help me through the first night at the Center, but you saved me from that creep at the Kinky Goat. You hold a special place in my heart, Baron. You always will." Old habits die hard, and she *almost* went up on her tiptoes to kiss those delicious lips. However, Brie fought the urge, concentrating instead on the reassuring weight of the collar around her neck.

"How long are you here, Brie?" Lea asked, spinning her around to face her.

Oh, how Brie had missed Lea's infectious enthusiasm. "Only a week, I think. Sir is a busy man and I don't think he'll have time to visit very long."

Master Anderson put his hand on her shoulder, his confident hold on her making Brie feel warm and tingly all over. "We'll take however much time we're given. Right now, however, Ms. Clark, Baron and I have some serious culling to do of the submissive entrants. Why don't you and Lea spend some time catching up while we make our determinations?"

"How many videos today?" Baron asked.

Master Anderson grinned. "Only seven, but we can only choose two more for this coming session."

Lea happily led her out of the conference room, but Brie glanced back and shivered involuntarily. To think that all the trainers at the Submissive Training Center had evaluated her own entrance video was a sobering thought.

It was a good thing she'd only imagined Sir watching it when she'd filmed her application or she would have lost her nerve. She looked briefly at Ms. Clark. What had the Domme thought when she'd viewed it? Had there been division among the trainers even then about her being part of the program?

Brie wondered if it was a blessing to be ignorant of the inner workings of a training center. Wise or not, she found herself hungry to know more and asked Lea, "Have you ever watched an entrance video?"

"Oh no—they're very strict about that. Only the trainers see them, then they're erased once the students have been chosen. They take the applicants' privacy very seriously."

"That's good to know…" As Lea led her down the hall to the Submissive Lounge, Brie asked a question that had been needling her. "Do they ever talk about what happens in those videos?"

"No, silly, I told you—they're very protective of the entries. It's serious business, girlfriend. Each applicant is treated with the same respect they give their students." She bumped Brie on the hip. "Why? Was there something in your submission video you're worried about? Come on, spill the beans!"

"Nothing too embarrassing, but you have to admit that thin little stick of a dildo was humorous to work with."

Lea giggled. "I bet they did that just to see if we could suck tiny dicks without laughing."

"Yeah, probably a requirement for admission to the

Center. You know…just in case," Brie added with an exaggerated wink. "I wonder what other subs do to make themselves stand out in their videos."

Lea answered with a wicked twinkle in her eye. "I cracked a couple of my famous jokes and showed off my gorgeous boobs when I did mine. I'm positive that's why I was picked. What about you?"

Brie blushed. "I…umm…cried out a certain Headmaster's name. Of course, I didn't know who he was at the time, but he certainly inspired my performance."

"OMG, Brie!" Lea put her arm around Brie's shoulders. "Tell me more, girlfriend."

"Let's just say that Sir Thane Davis told me it was one of the finest entries he's ever seen."

"I bet!"

Brie nervously confessed, "I just can't help wondering what Coen, Marquis and Clark thought when they saw it."

"If you cried out Sir's name, I'm sure he had a lot of explaining to do."

Brie frowned. "You're probably right, but how can I find out for sure?"

"Hey, here's a novel thought. Why don't you ask Sir? You know what they say, girlfriend. Communication is the cornerstone of a healthy D/s relationship."

"Yeah, yeah…" Brie conceded.

Lea dragged her to a couch and sat her down. "So tell me what happened in Japan. I was devastated to hear about Tono's father."

Brie quickly caught her up, but she purposely left out the confession Tono's father had made, as well as her disappointment that Tono was staying in Japan to care for his mother.

"So Tono can really sing, huh?"

"Oh yeah, Lea, you wouldn't believe it. He could sing professionally if he wanted to."

"Who knew the man was multitalented?"

"I know! Can you just imagine him and his father belting it out in secret?"

Lea shook her head. "No, I can't. I really can't."

"Well, I couldn't have either until I visited his father this last time. I saw a whole new side to him."

"That's good...and kind of sad."

Brie sighed. "Yes, it is. I didn't come to understand the man until he was dying."

"I came across a joke recently that made me think of Tono."

Brie knew that was Lea's way of trying to add some lightheartedness to a tough situation, so she sacrificed for the team. "Okay...let me hear it."

Lea squealed. "Great! You can share it with Tono, if you want, the next time you see him."

"I will, but only if it's funny."

"Of course it is! Do you know why I didn't enjoy my time at the bondage club last night?"

"No, Lea. Why didn't you enjoy your time at the bondage club last night?"

"All I wanted was sex with no strings attached."

Brie groaned. "Boo!"

"Ooh, ooh, I've got another one!"

"I'm not sure I can handle another one."

"Bondage is brilliant!" Lea exclaimed, wrapping her

arms tightly around herself. "Truss me."

Brie groaned as she shook her head. "Those were both terrible."

"But they made you smile," Lea insisted.

"Only because they were so bad."

"Exactly! That's the beauty of a good bad joke—you can't help but love them."

"The only thing I love is you. The jokes? Not so much."

"Aww, aren't you just the sweetest stinky cheese? Wait! I've got one more."

"No more, Lea. Please, no more."

"But this one's for you," she said, pouting.

Lea was hard to resist, so Brie relented against her better judgment. "Fine, but I'm only letting you because I love you."

"I love you too, Brie," she cooed, giving her a tight squeeze. "So…did you hear about the French cheese factory that exploded?"

"Nope."

"All that was left was de Brie."

This time Brie actually laughed.

"De Brie! Isn't that great?"

"It's stupid, but I love it," Brie admitted. "Thanks, Lea."

"Anytime, girlfriend. So what are your plans while you're here?"

"Well, I'm hoping to film a few scenes at the Academy. But mostly I just want to spend every minute I can hanging out with you."

"Me too! But…not tonight."

Brie was crushed. "Why not?"

"I already made plans with another friend."

"Can't I join you?"

Lea hesitated. "She's extremely shy, Brie. It's taken me weeks just to get her to agree to go out with me tonight."

Brie thought she understood and asked in a hushed tone, "Is she a new *girl*friend, by any chance?"

Lea rolled her eyes. "No, silly. She's a really cool person I want to know better but if I ask you to join us, she'll bail on me."

"But Lea," Brie whimpered, "I haven't seen you in like…forever. I'm only here for a week. *Please* don't leave me hanging tonight."

In answer, Lea gave Brie another squeeze. "I know this stinks, but if things go well tonight I'll ask if she'd like to meet you. I make no promises and you can't be offended if she says no."

Now it was Brie's turn to roll her eyes. "What, is this girl a mountain hermit or something?"

Lea hemmed and hawed before answering, "You could say that, I guess."

Her best friend was being so weird and secretive that it turned Brie off. Even if this mystery person agreed to meet, Brie wasn't sure she would like the girl. "I only have a week here," she reminded Lea.

"I know, I know! But remember, I had no idea you were coming until you threw off your hood today."

Brie giggled. "Oh, my goodness, wasn't that nuts?"

"Master Anderson is so bad!" Lea agreed. "It's another reason I love it here."

"Do you think Ms. Clark will forgive me? I was really surprised she handled it so well."

Lea suddenly became serious. "Although Mistress Clark still maintains her strict demeanor, around the staff she's been much more open and fun." Lea mused out loud, "It seems she's less tortured than before. I'm unsure if it's moving to Denver, Master Anderson's crazy antics or what, but whatever the reason, it's nice that others are getting to see the person I fell in love with."

Brie wondered if letting go of Rytsar Durov had been the biggest contributing factor for the change in the Domme's attitude. "Are the two of you finally an item now?"

Lea shrugged. "She's still trying to find her way. I don't think even *she* knows what she wants, but I'm willing to wait. In the meantime I'm having tons of fun getting to know the other Dominants and submissives in Denver. They're a friendly bunch, let me tell you."

Brie clasped her hand. "I'm happy to hear it. It sounds as if I'll have to be content with seeing you tomorrow, then." She stuck out her bottom lip and whimpered, "But I don't know how I'll survive."

Lea held out her little finger and grinned. "I promise to make it up to you—pinky swear." Brie wrapped her pinky around Lea's and they shook to seal the deal.

Baron peeked his head into the room. "Ms. Taylor, Master Anderson has requested that you return to the staff room."

Lea got up reluctantly. "I'm sorry I have to leave you, Brie."

"Don't concern yourself," Baron replied smoothly.

"I'm taking Miss Bennett to the Rocky Mountain Brewery while you attend the meeting."

Brie loved the idea of getting to spend time alone with Baron, and waved goodbye to her best friend. "I'll be fine, woman. Go have fun with all that behind-the-scenes stuff you do."

"Later, 'gator," Lea called, throwing a kiss before traipsing out of the room.

"So, kitten, which do you prefer—dark or light beer?"

"I like it dark," she answered with a cheeky grin.

"Indeed."

He took her to the local brewery within walking distance of the training facility. It was lovely to stroll beside the handsome Dom under the blue skies of Denver. "Do you like it here, Baron?"

"It's different from LA. I'd say it's more laid back and more outdoorsy, but the people seem genuine. Yeah, I like it well enough."

"But your heart's still in Los Angeles?" Brie asked, detecting a hint of sadness in his voice.

"I miss the places and things that remind me of Adrianna."

It hurt Brie's heart to know that Baron was missing his submissive. She could only imagine how she would feel if she ever lost Sir. "Do you mind me asking how she died?"

"No, kitten, but let's get a beer and sit down first."

When they entered the Rocky Mountain Brewery he ordered two of their darkest brew at the bar, then settled beside Brie at a booth near the window, sliding a glass over to her.

Baron took a long drink and licked off the foam that rested on his upper lip. It was casually sexy, an unintended effect that made it all that much more charming.

"You were saying?" Brie prompted.

"Adrianna…" He said her name in a wistful, anguished tone. "She was my dream made flesh. Sir Davis invited me to her graduation party and introduced us personally. I knew then that she was the one. Our courtship was quick, her submission unconditional." He looked up from his beer. "I knew the love of a good woman, and it is because of that I survived the aftermath of her death."

Brie was gutted to see the love and pain expressed in his hazel eyes. "What happened to her?"

"Wrong place, wrong time… Adrianna and I had gone to a late-night movie at our neighborhood theater. It was raining, so I went to get the car. Three hoodlums walked past Adrianna while she was waiting. They attempted to mug her, but when she wouldn't give up her purse they beat my baby unconscious. I pulled up to find her on the pavement, bloody and unresponsive. Although I rushed her to the hospital…" He paused, looking away when he added gruffly, "My baby never woke up."

Brie grasped his hand. "I'm so sorry, Baron."

He smiled sadly at her. "As penance for not being there when she needed me, I've dedicated my life to protecting other women from the scum of the Earth."

"So that's why you were at the Kinky Goat…"

"Yes, but the last thing I wanted to see was you

there."

Brie hung her head in shame. "It was a terrible mistake."

"You did nothing wrong, other than meet with your friends at a place you weren't familiar with. In some ways it was similar to what happened to my Adrianna—wrong place, wrong time."

"She must be so proud of you now. Proud of your strength to carry on, proud of the many women you've helped."

He furrowed his brow, his eyes dull with unresolved pain. "I hope she has forgiven me for not being there." He shook his head. "Every time I think of that night, I hear her crying out my name, trusting I would save her—but I never came."

Brie swallowed down the lump in her throat. "Adrianna wouldn't have blamed you. I only have to put myself in that situation to know how she felt. Although she would have been praying you'd come in time, she died knowing she'd see you again, and that would have brought her peace."

He blinked away the tears that welled up in his eyes, and took another draught of beer. "Thank you, kitten," he said hoarsely.

Brie nodded, picking up her glass. "Do you think you'll end up going back to LA?"

He shrugged his broad shoulders. "I'm uncertain at this point. Mentally I understand the benefits of moving on, but my heart does not. It's not an easy thing to do."

"Do you like being a trainer at the Denver Academy?"

He chuckled. "I do enjoy being in the trainer role. It's much less formal than the Submissive Training Center, but I appreciate Master Anderson's vision."

Brie grinned, nodding in agreement. "He's no Master Coen."

"No, he's not. However, they both have their place."

"Agreed."

"Whether it's fair or not, I will always compare the Headmasters I work under to Sir Davis."

"He was amazing in that role, wasn't he?" Brie agreed, squelching the guilt that threatened to rise.

"I was saddened to hear about his troubles."

Brie felt a chill run through her and she slowly put down her glass after taking a drink. "What do you mean?"

He stared at her for several moments before replying, "I'm talking about his mother, kitten."

She breathed an inward sigh of relief. "I'm telling you, that woman is insane! However, I admire how Sir handled the situation with her."

Baron's hazel eyes penetrated her with their intensity and she squirmed under his gaze. Had she said too much? Brie picked up her beer and sipped it nervously.

Thankfully, Master Anderson walked through the doors and straight over to their table. "Are you ready? It appears I'm to be your entertainment for the evening, young Brie."

Blast from the Past

"**D**on't feel you need to take me out, Master Anderson," Brie told him, as she jumped into his massive truck.

"It's the least I can do. After all, I was the one who wanted to keep your arrival under wraps. I'm responsible for the fact you have no friend to hang with tonight." He started up the vehicle then turned to her. "I'll show you some of my old haunts so you can get a native's feel for Denver."

Brie forced a smile. Although she was appreciative of his offer to entertain her, she would much rather have hung with Lea. However, she realized it was a rare chance to get to know the Dom on a more personal level, and readjusted her attitude. Even though Sir was good friends with Master Anderson, she knew practically nothing about the man other than the fact that he was a jokester, a skilled expert with the bullwhip and an excellent cook.

He drove her into Denver so she could admire, in passing, the tall buildings of the downtown area as well as the charm of horse-drawn carriages on the 16th Street mall, before taking her to an older neighborhood lined with tall trees.

He eventually parked in front of a magnificent Victorian home. Brie loved the inviting porch, the detailed trim, the lancet windows and the castle feel of its charming turret.

Master Anderson stared at it with a small grin playing across his lips. "I miss that house."

"So that's where you used to live?" she asked in surprise.

"Yes. I purchased it when it was in severe disrepair. I was young and had the energy and time to give it the care it deserved. After I'd finished restoring the extensive scrollwork and trim, I played with the inside. Still keeping to the Gothic style, I added a special room at the back for my…unique brand of entertainment." His eyes twinkled when he pointed to the left side of the residence. "Inside there is a secret door. How I enjoyed the surprised gasps from my submissives the first time I introduced them to what my friends affectionately called 'The Room'."

"Oh, I wish I could see it, Master Anderson. I can't help but wonder what the new owners think of your play room."

"They were told it was a private room I used as an office." He chuckled to himself. "I wonder if they can still hear the squeals of delight that regularly echoed in that room." Master Anderson's eyes drifted affectionately to the yard. "After the interior was complete, I started on the neglected garden."

Brie looked beyond the dark iron gate. He'd filled the front yard with bushes, each with its own unique pigment which made the garden colorful but definitely kept a masculine feel to it.

"Wow, your garden is actually as impressive as the house," she complimented.

"Thank you. I'm quite proud of my work."

"Do you regret giving this place up?"

He looked at Brie thoughtfully. "My new home has the space this one lacked. Although they appear to be polar opposites, both homes have a style that speaks to me."

"You are a complicated man, Master Anderson. A cowboy as a child, a carpenter as a young man and now Headmaster of a BDSM training school."

"You are missing an important part of the journey." He started up the truck and drove her back to visit the downtown area. He helped her out of his vehicle, then walked Brie through a thriving college campus. "Once the house was complete, I had time on my hands and an ambition to be my own boss, so I took classes at night to get my business degree."

She looked at him in amazement. "How did you find the time?"

He raised an eyebrow. "I was not tied down to a partner and only played with subs on an occasional basis. It left me with an abundance of time, and I am not a man to waste it." He pointed towards a large glass-and-brick building with the impressive Rockies as its backdrop.

"I took classes at night here. While it took longer to

get my business degree, it has all led me to where I am now. I was able to redesign the warehouse into the Academy, and I have the business background necessary to ensure its success. Of course, it doesn't hurt that Thane let me see the inner workings of the Training Center."

Brie felt a pang of remorse. Why did the mention of Sir's prior status as Headmaster always hurt her heart?

Master Anderson walked her between the campus buildings, down a pleasant path of new trees and budding flowers. He shared memories of the professors he'd learned under and classes he'd taken. Although much of what he shared made no sense to her, Brie enjoyed hearing the tone of his voice change when he talked about business and how what he learned played into his endeavors now. "I want our school to adapt to the market, reacting to the needs of the local community as they change. I invite change, as long we never lose sight of our fundamental purpose."

He led her to a small Italian restaurant, opening the bright red door with a gentlemanly flourish. "A favorite place of mine back in the da—"

She looked up at him and was surprised to see his face lose all color as a cute redhead with a large baby bump made her way out the door.

"Pardon me," the young woman murmured with a smile. Then she stopped short and said in astonishment, "Brad?"

Master Anderson stiffened upon hearing his name. He froze temporarily, taking time before he replied, "Amy, I never expected to run into you here."

The redhead blushed. "Well, I love the food and seem to crave it more these days." She rubbed her belly lovingly. "Thank you for introducing me to this place. I visit a least once a week now."

He looked at her warily, as if she were a poison to him. Brie's heart went out to Master Anderson as the awkward silence stretched, so she stuck out her hand. "Hi, I'm Brie."

The girl glanced briefly at Brie's collar before taking her hand. "Hi, Brie. I'm Amy. I was good friends with Brad when we were taking night classes together."

Master Anderson seemed to snap out of his stupor and spoke, "Yes, Amy and I spent many stimulating nights at my house. How have you been?" He looked at her stomach. "I notice you have a bun in the oven."

Amy laughed sweetly. "Yes, we do. A little girl, if the ultrasound proves to be right. I sure hope so, because the nursery is all pink and my mother already bought a ton of lacy outfits for her."

Brie saw a flash of pain flit across Master Anderson's face before he hid it with a casual smile. "I take it you're still with Troy."

Amy looked at him sadly, letting Brie know there was so much between them that wasn't being said.

"Yes." There was another uncomfortably long pause as Amy played with the ring on her finger. "Troy and I got married last year."

"I see."

Brie slipped her hand into Master Anderson's and squeezed it, offering him moral support.

"Looks as if you two didn't waste any time," she

teased Amy.

The redhead shrugged, caressing her stomach affectionately. "Who'd have guessed we'd be so compatible?"

Master Anderson tightened his hold on Brie's hand, almost hurting her with his grip. "Congratulations, Amy. Be sure to give your husband my best. I hope you'll excuse us, as Brie and I have a schedule to keep."

Amy's gaze drifted back to Brie's collar. "I'm sure the two of you have a wonderful evening planned." She gave Master Anderson a clumsy hug, her large stomach getting in the way. "It was wonderful to see you again, Brad. You look great, and it's such a joy to meet your girlfriend."

Master Anderson didn't correct Amy's mistake, so Brie made a bold move, saying as she kissed him on the cheek, "Mr. Anderson is in high demand these days. I'm a very lucky girl."

"Yes…I'm sure," Amy replied, turning a bright shade of red. She added as she hurried off, "Have a great evening, you two." She looked back briefly before disappearing around the corner.

Master Anderson watched her go with a look of regret on his face. "I don't feel hungry. Do you mind if we head back to my place?"

"Not at all, Master Anderson."

The drive back was unbearably silent. Brie had never seen the Dom unraveled before. Her heart ached for him, but it was not her place to ask about the girl, so she stared out of the window admiring the snowy peaks in the distance.

Sir texted her as they waited in traffic. *How's my sexy*

submissive?

Brie smiled when she saw his message and told Master Anderson, "It's Sir. Do you mind if I text him back?"

"Please. I'm sure he misses you."

The sadness in his voice was not lost on her. "Thank you, Master Anderson."

She quickly typed, *I'm good, Sir. How are you?*

Doing well. In a couple of days I'll be better.

Why?

You'll be in my arms.

Brie squeaked, which caught Master Anderson's attention, so she explained, "Sir's coming here in a few days."

"That's good to hear. Tell him hello from me."

Brie dutifully typed, *Master Anderson says hi.*

I assumed you would be with Lea tonight, Brie.

She's busy, so Master Anderson took me on a tour of Denver.

Is he taking good care of my sub?

Of course, but do you have any idea who Amy is?

He took his time before texting back. *Why?*

Master Anderson met her today and seems extremely sad now.

I have an assignment for you, téa.

Yes, Master.

When you get off the phone, pull your skirt up and play with yourself.

It was Brie's turn to hesitate.

He continued to type. *Make yourself orgasm. Be vocal about it.*

??? She texted in surprise.

Trust your Master. Hang up now and do as I say.

Brie put the phone away and sighed, building up her courage. She hiked her skirt up, not daring to look in Master Anderson's direction.

With tentative fingers, she started to caress her pussy through her panties. It didn't take long for her body to react to the pleasurable sensation. She moaned a little, shifting to get a better angle. She could feel Master Anderson's eyes on her.

Brie slipped her hand under the wet material and swirled her finger over her clit. With a teasing motion she rubbed the sensitive area more rapidly and purred. Here they were in the middle of rush-hour traffic and she was playing with herself... Thankfully she was safe from the majority of prying eyes because of the height of his truck.

Master Anderson said nothing as he watched the road—and her.

Brie closed her eyes, arching her back, forcing her fingers inside as she imagined the head of Sir's cock penetrating her. He fucked her slowly, wanting her to feel and appreciate the full length of his shaft. Then she pulled her fingers out and rapidly rubbed her hungry clit.

The combination of penetration and clit play always brought on a delicious orgasm. She adjusted herself, putting a leg up on the dash for freer access. She needed deeper penetration, so she thrust her fingers more aggressively. The lace panties made it a little more difficult, but also added an element of naughtiness. With the angle he had, Master Anderson couldn't see what she was doing but he could certainly imagine it.

There finally came a point when the increasing fire between her legs transformed into pulses, letting her know an orgasm was near. She pressed her fingers hard against her clit and began to rub at a furious pace.

Her cries of passion filled the cabin of the truck as she gave in to the intensity of her self-made orgasm. "Oh, oh, ooohhh…" she moaned as it crashed over her. She felt her pussy contract in waves of pleasure. Afterwards she pressed her hand over her sex, enjoying those last little delicious pulses.

Without looking in Master Anderson's direction, she righted herself, pulling her skirt down and folding her hands in her lap.

"Your Master told you to do that?"

She looked at him shyly. "Yes, Master Anderson."

Brie was glad to see him smile for the first time since the unexpected meeting with Amy. "Leave it to Thane to know just what I needed. Well done, young Brie."

She smiled back. "I'm glad you approve, Master Anderson."

He raised his eyebrow. "You know I love watching a woman pleasure herself."

Brie blushed, thrilled that her little performance had been pleasing to him.

Maser Anderson drove high into the foothills, pulling off the road at a turnabout which gave them a spectacular view of Denver. He turned off the truck, staring at the sprawling city below. Without being asked, he shared, "I met Amy in a communications class. I knew the moment I laid eyes on her that I was meant to tame her."

"Tame her?" Brie asked, unfamiliar with the term.

He answered with a smirk. "Back then I loved the challenge of taking a strong woman unused to kink and showing her the excitement of submission. I affectionately refer to them as the 'wild ones', those women who don't realize their true nature—yet."

"So you liked educating totally vanilla girls?"

"Yes. However, Amy was different. That redheaded vixen intrigued me more than my previous conquests, and she proved far more resistant. Took me longer to tame her than any I'd had before, but when she finally submitted—*truly* submitted—I was lost."

"Lost how?" Brie asked, deeply honored that he was being so open with her.

"Amy broke my heart," Master Anderson stated with a sad half-smile. "Although I'd always enjoyed conquering wild ones, she was the first and only one to conquer me. I didn't realize how deeply I'd fallen until that ass came into the picture."

"Who?"

Master Anderson spat out the name disdainfully, "Troy Dawson."

"Is that her husband?"

Master Anderson snarled. "That selfish bastard doesn't deserve her. He was always making her cry, leaving her to chase his dreams then coming back, expecting her to welcome him with open arms. He didn't love her like I did. Damn it, I would have done anything for Amy. In fact…" His voice trailed off and he just stared at the horizon, lost in his painful memories.

Brie said nothing, instinctively putting her hand on his shoulder to express her empathy.

"I lost a part of myself the day she walked away from me. No explanation—she just walked into his arms and we were no more. But as hurt as I was, I never stopped loving the girl and willingly played the fool again when I saw an opportunity to win her back."

Brie couldn't imagine Master Anderson ever playing the fool and stated, "I don't believe it."

"I hate to admit it, but I ran to Amy's side when I heard she was seriously hurt. It was no surprise to me that Troy was nowhere to be found."

Master Anderson paused, a hint of regret in his voice when he added, "I did things I'm not proud of. Have you ever loved someone so desperately you compromised yourself to keep them?"

He looked critically at Brie for a moment, then answered his own question. "No, you haven't. That isn't your nature."

"What did you do?" Brie asked, intrigued that the Dom had found himself in such a position. "I can't imagine you ever compromising yourself."

"No one is immune to life's lessons, young Brie. Looking back on it now, I understand what a fool I was, but back then I justified my actions. She was mine—she'd freely given her submission to me. I also knew she needed to stay far away from that miserable excuse of a man. When fate saw fit to erase her memories, I took it as a sign. It was my second chance and I wasn't going to allow anything or *anyone* to fuck it up."

"What happened?" Brie prodded, now even more curious.

"I chose not to mention that she'd ever known Troy

Dawson. Why would I? I wanted to protect her from that asshole."

"So you did it because you loved her?"

"Yes. If Amy hadn't returned my feelings, I never would've been so persistent, nor would I have asked her to marry me. I tell you, young Brie—the day she accepted my proposal, I'd never felt so happy, didn't know it was possible to feel that level of joy."

He snarled in frustration. "Naturally, that's when *he* showed up. Troy always returned just when she was getting her life back together. I tried to warn her that he was no good, but her heart was set."

Master Anderson stared out at the city, sighing deeply. "When she turned me down that second time, I was done." He added in a low, angry growl, "But to see her now. To see her heavy with child, with *his* child... It should have been mine."

Tears came to Brie's eyes as she realized how hurt he was. Although Master Anderson was a strong, confident Dom, he was still human. They sat in the truck, silently watching two black starlings swoop and twist in the orange sky as the sun set.

His next words were heartbreaking, and something Brie would never forget. "What I had failed to appreciate was that I had won her submission and love, but I never had her heart."

She wrapped her arms around his muscular shoulders. "I'm sorry your heart was broken by your first love."

He stated with conviction, "I will never be that weak again."

Brie replied with equal conviction, "Master Anderson, I believe true love makes you strong—not weak."

He stared at her for several seconds before giving her a hint of a smile. "Spoken like a sage. I suppose I still hold out hope of finding what you share with Thane. That's why his little stunt tonight was perfect. I needed to be reminded there are subs who love their Masters and remain completely devoted to them."

"Your sub is out there, Master Anderson," Brie declared. "She's just waiting to rock your world."

He chuckled. "You never knew this, but I was concerned for Thane when I first met you. His obsession reminded me of my own. I was certain my friend would suffer the same fate I had."

Brie proclaimed proudly, "We are condors, Sir and I."

Master Anderson appeared amused by her statement. "You *do* realize condors are vultures? They eat the meat of rotting animals."

Brie giggled. "They do, but they also mate for life."

"Lots of animals mate for life. You could have chosen swans, wolves or even turtle doves." He shook his head, chuckling under his breath. "Why condors, of all things?"

Brie was not offended by his teasing and happily enlightened him. "The condor is the perfect choice, Master Anderson. While the world concentrates on what they perceive as our flaws, we focus only on each other. They will never know the beauty we see every day."

The amusement on his face faded. "That's profound, young Brie."

Master Anderson started up the truck again. "I've suddenly had a change of heart. Let's go clubbing tonight, vanilla style."

Brie squealed as he peeled out of the turnabout and headed back down the mountain.

Wicked King

Brie woke up in a panic. She glanced around the unfamiliar bedroom, struggling to remember where she was. It took several moments before her heart stopped racing, once she realized she was at Master Anderson's.

The frightening dream which had awakened her was already disappearing into the murky recesses of her mind, but she felt certain that Sir's mother, Ruth, had been part of it.

She shook off the unpleasant aftereffects of the dream and hurried to the shower to begin her day. When she returned to her room, Brie was pleasantly surprised to find her fantasy journal lying on the bed. She picked it up, along with the note beside it.

Your Master wants to read a new fantasy, téa. ~ Sir

Brie flipped through the pages of her beloved journal, realizing that Sir must have had it shipped to Master Anderson's house from their apartment. It'd been a while since she'd written in its pages—far too long. There were so many wonderful memories wrapped up in that little book; from her very first fantasy, which Rytsar had made into delicious reality during her auction, to her Sun God fantasy that Boa managed to fulfill with his gargantuan cock. Then there was her Naughty King fantasy, which Sir had played out as Khan just before Graduation Day.

She pressed the book against her chest, thrilled to be holding it again, and whispered, "Thank you, Sir."

Brie curled up on the bed and began to write, grateful there was no time constraint this time as she began to pen her fantasy.

"Stop. Step away from her."

The priest moves away from me. The relief on his face would be insulting, but I understand why. He's grateful that he will not have to break his vows to God to prove his loyalty to our King.

I am relieved as well, pleased to have my virginity still intact.

"Girl."

The men holding me down release my wrists. I get up slowly, straightening my skirt with shaking hands.

"Retire to my room," my King orders. "I will partake of you later."

I bow to him, honored to have been granted such a privilege. I glance up to see the proud look on my father's face. I'm escorted from the great hall and led through the castle. All the splendor and wealth displayed on the walls gives me hope. Surely after tonight, the King will forgive our family's debt.

The guards lead me to a section of the castle that few are allowed to enter. The King's room is covered in large, intricate tapestries depicting his many battles over the years. I look around, flattered that my virginity will be given to such a great man.

The next few hours are spent with attendants as they ready me for the King. After a thorough bath and cleaning, I am covered in sweet-smelling perfume. My hair is curled and tied up into a traditional bun, which signifies my virginal status.

I'm then dressed in a white, gossamer gown. The thin material lightly brushes against my nipples as it slides down and settles into place. I feel like a princess, a beautiful princess about to be taken by her handsome King.

Two men enter the King's chamber. "So this is the one?" the younger of the two asks.

"Yes."

"A virgin?"

"That is what she claims," the other replies.

"I'm required to check." When the young one approaches me, I freeze. "I will not hurt you, child," he says reassuringly as his hand disappears under my gown. I stiffen when I feel his finger press against my mound. "Open your legs, girl."

I look to the other man, who nods. I reluctantly move my feet apart and gasp as his finger presses against my tiny opening.

"By God, she's tight". He switches fingers, penetrating me with his pinky. It is the first time I have ever felt such an invasion and I whimper with discomfort.

"You break that hymen and it'll be your head," the other man growls.

The first man removes his finger and looks hungrily at me. "I would love to watch this one lose her virginity."

"You can, for a price," the other states proudly.

"How?"

"The risk is considerable, but it can be done."

The man looks me over again. "I'll pay it, whatever the cost. I want to hear her scream."

I ignore the two men, disgusted by their behavior. However, they have foolishly given me valuable information. Should the King prove ungenerous, I can blackmail them to guarantee my family's survival.

"It'll be worth the considerable price, my friend," the older man assures him. "The King has particular tastes when it comes to virgins."

Two other girls enter the room upon his words, followed by an imposing eunuch. The young maidens are dressed in identical white gowns.

The older male smiles lewdly as he explains to his partner, "Our Majesty likes to take them three at a time."

The eunuch holds rope in his hand. He takes the wrists of the girl closest to him and ties her hands together before guiding her to the giant bed. We all watch as he orders her to kneel on the edge of it. He makes quick work of binding her so her legs are spread and her arms secure.

He motions to the other girl. She glides over to the bed and willingly offers her hands to him. He grunts in satisfaction as he trusses the second girl beside the first. He looks up at me next, holding up the last of the rope.

My heart races as I approach; I know there is no escape from my fate once I am bound. I glance briefly at the door but know my choice is already made.

I hold up my wrists to him. My heart skips a beat as he wraps them in the rope, then directs me to kneel on the bed like the other two girls. With competent hands he spreads my legs and binds them, securing me to the frame of the bed. I struggle in my bonds, testing their strength.

"You aren't going anywhere," the eunuch informs me arrogantly.

All three men exit, leaving us young girls alone in the King's chamber. The other two are as silent as I am, probably contemplating what the night ahead holds for us.

I'm frightened. I will no longer be innocent after tonight, but there is another part of me that longs to become a woman in the arms of my King. Despite my eagerness, I jump like a scared rabbit when I hear his voice just outside the door. He enters and chuckles to himself when he sees the three of us. I hear the swish of fabric as he is undressed by his manservant.

"Leave me," he orders, and I hear the man make a quick exit.

We are now alone with our King…

I watch through veiled eyes as he ties a gag over the mouth of the virgin farthest away from me. The other girl and I tense as our King places his large hands on her buttocks. My view of his manhood is obstructed, but based on the girl's stifled moans, our King has an impressive cock.

Her muffled cry announces her entrance into womanhood.

Our King grunts as he thrusts into her, making me tremble with fearful excitement. I have guarded my maidenhead diligently to ensure my future as a bride, but now I will be giving it away to my King.

He pulls out and moves to the next girl. Another sash comes out and he gags her. This girl whimpers when he starts pressing into her. He slaps her ass hard, the sound of it echoing through the expansive chamber. "Quiet."

She closes her eyes and is completely silent when he begins to thrust. He growls with passion. "Move with me."

My King groans in satisfaction as he takes her more deeply. I cannot stop shaking, knowing my turn is approaching. In just a few moments I will be a woman in every sense of the word…

I gasp involuntarily when he pulls out of her and grabs my ass with both hands.

"Desperate for your King, are you?"

I nod, surprised when he does not gag me like the others.

"You have not been raised for this like the other girls. I shall savor your maidenhead that much more."

I look back at him, becoming entranced by his lustful stare. Being desired by a man is a new and intoxicating experience for me and I find I'm no longer resentful of my father—I desire my King to have my virginity for purely selfish reasons.

I purr in pleasure when he undoes my bun and lets my long hair fall over my back. Then he wraps his hand in my silky tresses and pulls my head back. I feel his hard shaft pressing against my tight opening, and whimper in fear and anticipation, knowing my moment is at hand.

"Remember this night, girl."

I start to pant as he forces himself inside me. My body is resistant even though I desperately want to feel the fullness of him. I push against his shaft, hoping to break through my virginal resistance, but he slaps my ass in protest.

"Stay still."

I do not move and my whole world expands as I relax, allowing his Kingly shaft to open me up. The pain is replaced with wonder when he begins to stroke me with his manhood. Nothing else exists but the two of us as I revel in this new connection.

Closing my eyes, I concentrate on the sensation of his shaft forcing itself deeper. Oh, this wondrous feeling of being utterly possessed!

I'm saddened when he pulls out, and cry, "More, my King."

He seems amused by my heartfelt plea. "Are you begging, girl?" Slapping my pink ass, he replies, "I have already taken your virginity—what else of value do you have for your King?"

"I would give you anything," I answer confidently as he bends down and bites my shoulder, his rigid shaft pressing against me.

"Anything?"

"Yes."

He takes his manhood in his hand and repositions it against my forbidden hole.

I can't breathe, taken by complete surprise by his demand.

"Are you still as willing?" he challenges.

I'm shocked by my own answer. "Yes, my King."

He covers my mouth with one hand, while grabbing my ass with the other. This possession will not be like the first.

"Give in to me, girl. Don't resist."

Although I am frightened, I imagine his shaft deep inside me and my body responds favorably. The round head of his cock breaches my entrance and I groan into his hand. My ass aches as I take his length.

My breath comes in gasps when he begins to move inside me. I feel dirty and yet delightfully wicked being taken this way by him.

My King's muscles tense as he forces himself farther into my darkness.

I am now completely and utterly His.

Brie put down the pen and sighed with unreleased need. She wondered what Sir would think when he read about the return of the King. She flipped through the pages again, noting that this fantasy was much longer than the others in her journal. Having been given unlimited time, she'd been able to fully detail her fantasy while still leaving her Master leeway to take it wherever he desired.

What will Sir do with this particular fantasy? Brie wondered. It had elements of Lea's birthday gift with the addition of other girls, while continuing the Khan fantasy he'd played out with her just before Graduation. This time, however, it included one of his favorite pastimes—her ass.

Brie kissed her beloved journal before slipping it into the overnight envelope. Although she was grateful for the connection that writing her fantasy had given her, it also made her miss Sir that much more.

She decided that must be the life of a condor—the continuous longing and need for the other. While some might see it as a weakness, she saw it as part of their strength. When they were separated, each of them was still strengthened by the knowledge that the other was thinking of them and impatient to reunite. Then, when they finally came back together, the intensity of the union seemed that much more powerful.

Brie hugged the package one more time before dropping it into Master Anderson's mailbox. She felt a thrill of excitement, knowing her journal was headed off to her Master.

How will Sir make her Wicked King fantasy come true?
Find out in, *Surprise Me.*

Buy the next in the series:

#1 (Teach Me)

#2 (Love Me)

#3 (Catch Me)

#4 (Try Me)

#5 (Protect Me)

#6 (Hold Me)

#7 (Surprise Me)

#8 (Trust Me)

Brie's Submission series:

Red Phoenix is the author of:

Blissfully Undone
* Available in eBook and paperback
(Snowy Fun—Two people find themselves snowbound in a cabin where hidden love can flourish, taking one couple on a sensual journey into ménage à trois)

His Scottish Pet: Dom of the Ages
* Available in eBook and paperback
Audio Book: *His Scottish Pet: Dom of the Ages*
(Scottish Dom—A sexy Dom escapes to Scotland in the late 1400s. He encounters a waif who has the potential to free him from his tragic curse)

The Erotic Love Story of Amy and Troy
* Available in eBook and paperback
(Sexual Adventures—True love reigns, but fate continually throws Troy and Amy into the arms of others)

eBooks

Varick: The Reckoning

(Savory Vampire—A dark, sexy vampire story. The hero navigates the dangerous world he has been thrust into with lusty passion and a pure heart)

Keeper of the Wolf Clan (Keeper of Wolves, #1)

(Sexual Secrets—A virginal werewolf must act as the clan's mysterious Keeper)

The Keeper Finds Her Mate (Keeper of Wolves, #2)

(Second Chances—A young she-wolf must choose between old ties or new beginnings)

The Keeper Unites the Alphas (Keeper of Wolves, #3)

(Serious Consequences—The young she-wolf is captured by the rival clan)

Boxed Set: Keeper of Wolves Series (Books 1-3)

(Surprising Secrets—A secret so shocking it will rock Layla's world. The young she-wolf is put in a position of being able to save her werewolf clan or becoming the reason for its destruction)

Socrates Inspires Cherry to Blossom

(Satisfying Surrender—a mature and curvaceous woman becomes fascinated by an online Dom who has much to teach her)

By the Light of the Scottish Moon

(Saving Love—Two lost souls, the Moon, a werewolf and a death wish…)

In 9 Days

(Sweet Romance—A young girl falls in love with the new student, nicknamed 'the Freak')

---

9 Days and Counting

(Sacrificial Love—The sequel to In 9 Days delves into the emotional reunion of two longtime lovers)

And Then He Saved Me

(Saving Tenderness—When a young girl tries to kill herself, a man of great character intervenes with a love that heals)

Play With Me at Noon

(Seeking Fulfillment—A desperate wife lives out her fantasies by taking five different men in five days)

Connect with Red on Substance B

Substance B is a platform for independent authors to directly connect with their readers. Please visit Red's Substance B page where you can:

- Sign up for Red's newsletter
- Send a message to Red
- See all platforms where Red's books are sold

Visit Substance B today to learn more about your favorite independent authors.

CPSIA information can be obtained
at www.ICGtesting.com
Printed in the USA
LVOW04s1958211016
509751LV00008B/419/P